For John,
who unluckily did not live
to see his egg hatch

THE INCREDIBLE LUCK OF ALFIE PLUCK

Jamie Rix

First published 2010 by
Orion Children's Books,
a division of
the Orion Publishing Group Ltd
This Large Print edition published
2011 by AudioGO Ltd
by arrangement with
the Orion Publishing Group Ltd

ISBN: 978 1405 664905

British Library Cataloguing in Publication Data available

Printed and bound in Great Britain by
CPI Antony Rowe, Chippenham and Eastbourne

CHAPTER ONE

If ever a boy needed some luck it was Alfie Pluck.

His ears stuck out like jug handles, his hair resembled a coconut and looked like the barber had employed a beaver to gnaw its way around the edges, and he was very short for an eleven-year-old. Instead of having parents, he had two greedy aunts, Hecate and Mohana, who had taken him into their dingy yellow house, brought him up at great personal expense, and never let him forget it. Their sacrifices came at a cost, which they extracted mercilessly.

At the age of two, having just taken his first faltering steps, they sent him off to the shops on his own to buy fish and chips for their supper. At the age of three, the second his hands were big enough for oven gloves, they set him to work in the kitchen baking their beloved Squashed-Fly biscuits. At the age of four, when he was old enough to feel guilty, they blamed him for robbing them of their beauty. It was only because of looking after him that they had lost their glow and never married.

From then on they gave him the full-time job of Household Drudge, which involved a little bit of housework and an awful lot of making his aunts look beautiful again. They taught him how to pluck hairs out of their legs with a pair of pliers, clean out their ears with newspaper and vinegar and shave off their corns with a cheese-grater.

And because Alfie had never known any other way of life, he stayed where he was and did as he was told. It never crossed his mind to run away, because his aunts had told him what would happen if he did. On the common there lived a pack of werefoxes, supernatural creatures of the night that could read the thoughts of bad children. They would infiltrate his dreams, learn of his plans to escape, snatch him as he left the house and eat him.

And so it was, on this particular day, that Alfie was hungry and there was no money for food, because his aunts had spent their last few pennies on a mud-bath pack.

'The cupboard is bare, boy!' hissed Mohana. 'Stop wearing out the hinges opening and closing that wretched larder door.' The two overweight aunts, dressed in their favourite pink frills, and looking like two ugly-fruits at a plum wedding, were sitting at the table flicking through a stack of well-thumbed wedding magazines.

'If you're hungry and want money to eat,

go out and earn it,' snarled Hecate. 'You're eleven years old. What's wrong with you?'

'And while you're out there,' sneered Mohana, prodding Alfie towards the front door with her long, sharp fingernails, 'buy something lovely for us too!'

Alfie was glad to get out of the house. Outside the confines of 13 Mire Road he could pretend he was free. Thrusting his hands into the pockets of his shorts, he wandered slowly down to the High Street. A discarded copy of yesterday's *Daily Sneer* was poking out of the bin outside Chango's Chicken Shack. There was a picture of a bald man on the front cover and a headline that caught his eye.

THE DAILY SNEER
Tuesday April 11th

IT'S YOUR CLUCKY DAY!
[By Entertainment Correspondent — Lily Quick]
Dr Leviticus Shard arrives in London today to the type of welcome usually reserved for pop stars. He claims to have discovered the elusive Luck Gene and

in the process created the luckiest chicken in the world.

'It's only a matter of time,' he says excitedly, 'before Luck in a Bottle is on sale in every high street in the land!'

He is due to demonstrate his bonkers discovery outside the posh-as-peas Dorchester Hotel in swanky Park Lane. Hen is it all happening? At 12.30pm tomorrow. The nearest tube is La-Di-Da Central. Chick it out!

Luck in a Bottle! The very idea made Alfie smile. If he had even the tiniest shred of luck in his bones, he'd look back at his aunt's house now and see a runaway bulldozer ploughing through the front door, razing the building to the ground and flattening everyone inside! He retraced his steps and peered round the corner, but no such luck. Still, Park Lane would be a good place to earn some money. There was bound to be a crowd, and where there were people there was business.

4

*　　　*　　　*

Park Lane was a six-lane carriageway in the heart of London's Mayfair. The idea of a Luck Gene had clearly captured the public's imagination, because the road was busy. Alfie positioned himself at the traffic lights opposite the Dorchester Hotel with a sponge and bucket that he'd 'borrowed' from a breakfasting window cleaner. Alfie was nothing if not inventive. From here he could not only ambush sitting-duck motorists and wash their windscreens whether they liked it or not, but he could also watch Dr Shard's historic demonstration at the same time.

First, though, he deserved a little rest. At home, time off was a luxury that Hecate and Mohana forbade, so sitting outside in the sunshine was a rare pleasure. He laid the newspaper out on the pavement, sat down on top of an article about the first British Space Mission, and closed his eyes.

GOING TO THE DOG STAR!

[By Science Correspondent—Tessa Tube)

The British Space Programme hit another glitch today when the Microwave Oven on board the Shuttle *Relentless* blew up, leaving the astronauts without any means of re-heating their food. Luckily, Mission Control, from its top secret headquarters in the O2 Centre (formerly The Millennium Dome) has the answer. If the astronauts can force themselves to swallow their packets of dried food, drink a pint of water and jump up and down for ten minutes the food will naturally rehydrate in

6

their stomachs and deliver all the nutrients they need.

Mmmm. Yummy!

This is another embarrassment for the Prime Minister, Marjorie Lentless, who has pushed through this first British moon mission with money that critics say could have been better spent on hospitals, schools and jobs. Since its launch three days ago, the mission has been dogged by bad luck, losing an engine because of some nesting fieldmice, orbiting the wrong way round the earth because an engineer had installed the vidiscreen upside down, and setting a course for Saturn after the Planet Recognition System mistook it for the moon.

                    *   *   *

Alfie woke with a start to find that he had been swallowed up by a large crowd. He jumped to his feet and pushed through a forest of people to the edge of the road where he was surprised to see that the traffic was still flowing freely. The police normally stopped cars for major events.

Not this time,' explained a know-it-all in the crowd. 'Apparently the traffic is a crucial part of the doctor's demonstration.'

As Alfie watched the posse of journalists and photographers who had assembled in front of The Dorchester, he saw a black limousine cruise to a halt and the Prime Minister, a lady with a brisk step and a helmet of cement-coloured hair, step out. She was accompanied by her newly appointed Minister for Good News, the natty, if slightly nervous, Cecil de Blouson. The Prime Minister waved to the crowd, who booed her enthusiastically. Then a second car arrived and Alfie recognised Dr Shard, who was ejected from the vehicle carrying a cage containing his lucky chicken.

On the other side of the road, with cars flashing past his nose, Alfie crossed his arms and waited for history to be made.

*   *   *

The Prime Minister kicked off proceedings with what Alfie understood to be a typical politician's speech. She made it *sound* as if she was only concerned about everybody else, whereas in fact she was only concerned about herself

'Ladies and gentlemen,' she said. 'It's impossible for me to know each and every one of you individually, but I feel as if I do. *Your* pain is *my* pain, and *my* success at the general election will be *your* success too. Now I know that you are all fed up with this nasty recession that has gobbled up your money and smashed your dreams to smithereens. I know how you're feeling, because I feel the same. That is why we are all here today, isn't it? Hoping that a little bit of this chicken's luck will rub off on us. I certainly am. Like you, I want things to be better too. And it's because of my sensitivity to your needs that this country's future, as we approach a General Election, is safe in my hands.'

'Is that why you've wasted millions of taxpayers' money sending a rocket to the moon?' shouted a female voice from the crowd.

'Oh dear,' muttered the Minister for Good News. 'There's going to be a riot.'

The Prime Minister tipped her head to one side and pulled her face into a serious frown.

'Let me answer the lady by asking her a question,' she said, turning defence into attack. 'Why are we here today? I'll tell you why. Because Dr Shard *believed*. He believed that there was something better out there and he didn't stop until he'd found it. The same applies to my moon mission. It is a glorious adventure that will one day prove that I was right to do everything I did.'

Meanwhile, Dr Shard was not a young man and the chicken in the cage under his arm was getting heavy.

'Can we hurry up, please?' he said out loud. Even Alfie heard it from across the street.

Clearly irritated, the Prime Minister turned back to the crowd and announced rather briskly,

'We are here today to celebrate the greatest breakthrough in science since the discovery of the genome. Dr Leviticus Shard has isolated Gene 1684327, otherwise known as the Luck Gene. Dr Shard.'

As the doctor stepped forward, the woman in the crowd shouted out a second question that had the Prime Minister clambering back to the microphone.

'I'd have thought that dispensing good luck on the streets would be a handy tool for the most unpopular Prime Minister in living memory, wouldn't you?'

'Who are you?' snapped Mrs Lentless.

'Lily Quick from the *Daily Sneer.*'

The Prime Minister smiled as if that explained the rudeness.

'Well, Lily Quick, popularity is not something I care about.'

Alfie knew a liar when he saw one. The PM continued, 'I do care, however, about everyone in the world having good luck, because that's the sort of person I am.'

'Nobody believes that, Prime Minister. Ever since the Shuttle *Relentless* started malfunctioning like an elephant's rollerskate your name has become synonymous with an expensive flop. You're bottom of the polls and careering towards the biggest election defeat in modern history.'

The Minister for Good News decided this was the right time to step between his incandescent boss and the microphone.

'The Prime Minister is not here to discuss the election,' he said. 'This is a good news story.' At which point somebody threw an egg which splattered all over the Prime Minister's coat.

11

Dr Shard lurched forward and dropped his caged chicken on the ground.

'I can't hold this any longer,' he grumbled irritably, taking control of the microphone as the PM attempted to wipe her coat. 'Anyway, we're here to listen to *me* not *her*. All my life I've been telling people like Marjorie Lentless that if I could harness the power of luck the world would be a better place, and all my life people like Marjorie Lentless have been telling me that I'm mad.'

Alfie could see why. With clumps of long black hair flapping above his ears like a raven's wings, cracked spectacles and over-expressive arms, Dr Shard did indeed look a little unhinged. Pockets of the crowd started to laugh at him.

'You won't be laughing at me when you see what I've created,' he shouted. 'You'll be sick with jealousy when I'm the richest man in the world!'

'Get on with it!' cried a lone distant voice.

Alfie thought the doctor was going to jump into the crowd and sort them out one by one. Fortunately a security guard stepped forward to restrain him. The doctor shook his arms free, smoothed down his wings of hair and took a deep, calming breath.

'Five years ago,' he proclaimed, 'I took one hundred hens' eggs to the top of a tall building and dropped them off the roof into the street. One egg survived the fall. I called it my Lucky Egg and hatched it into a Lucky Hen, who laid another hundred eggs, which I took to the top of the same building and dropped over the edge. This time *three* Lucky Eggs survived. So I hatched three Lucky Hens who laid another hundred eggs and *eight* survived, and so on and so on. Eventually, every egg survived the fall and I had one hundred Lucky Hens!

'Unfortunately, that night, a fox broke into the hen house and ate ninety-nine of them. At first I was distraught, but then I realised that the fox had done me a favour, because it had got rid of the impostors. There was only ever *one* Lucky Hen and now I had found it.'

As Dr Shard bent to pick up the cage, the crowd held its breath in expectation. Alfie's head was telling him that this mad doctor was a cheap fraud, but in his heart he wanted him to be right.

Imagine a world with luck on tap. Lucky Alfie wouldn't have to be a Household Drudge any more. He could unchain his three-legged dog, Bandit, from the hut in the garden and they could run away. He could take his chances on the street, unafraid of werefoxes, and do whatever it took to get by. He could sell ice creams. And when he was rich and famous he would find himself a proper family, who ate supper together, went on holidays and owned a dishwasher.

An ear-piercing squawk broke Alfie's reverie and snapped his attention back to the stage.

'Meet Henrietta,' announced Dr Shard, opening the door of the cage.

Alfie leaned forward with the rest of the expectant crowd as the doctor grabbed Henrietta by her feet and dragged her out. He swung his arm around his head. 'This is what luck looks like,' he shouted excitedly. As he released his grip on the screeching bird, it tumbled into the air, flapped its useless wings and landed untidily on the road in the middle of the traffic.

Instinctively Alfie moved forward to save it.

'Don't!' cried the doctor. 'The hen will not be harmed!'

That was hard to believe, but even so the chicken appeared unmoved by the clamour around it; the screeching tyres, the choking exhaust pipes, the horns and general commotion of cars and people panicking.

14

It just walked calmly towards the other side of the road, stopping occasionally to peck at a dead fly on the tarmac. And, miraculously, the cars didn't hit it. They swerved and braked, but the hen, it seemed, was surrounded by an invisible force field of luck.

If Alfie could choose one Christmas present (not that he would be allowed to, because his aunts believed that giving presents to children only encouraged pleasure, which in turn begat idleness) an invisible force field of luck would be top of his list.

Suddenly, behind Alfie, there was a surge in the crowd as people struggled for a better view. He was shoved in the back and, along with several other spectators, pushed forward into the road in front of a yellow London taxi. The cab swerved and flashed past Alfie, mere inches from his nose. It was so close he could see every crease in the driver's face, which was framed by a lank mop of straight black hair. Wide, staring eyes were fixed in horror on a spot in front of his bonnet.

The cab caught the Lucky Hen a glancing blow with its bumper. The chicken was hurled into the air like an exploding feather-football and landed with a grateful thud in Alfie's outstretched arms.

The world seemed to trip into slow-motion.

*   *   *

Alfie heard a cry go up from the stage.

'Seize that boy!' It was Dr Shard. 'SEIZE THAT BOY!'

But a crowd is a big, unwieldy beast and takes a moment to respond. Individual faces, shocked and confused, turned to look at him, but as a group they did nothing. 'FIND SOME ICE!' came the desperate voice from the stage. 'KEEP THAT DEAD HEN COLD TILL I CAN CUT OUT ITS BRAIN.'

But the hen wasn't dead. Alfie could feel it stirring in his arms. The blow from the taxi had merely stunned it. Clearly, it wasn't a Lucky Hen for nothing.

Now the frozen world suddenly came flooding back. As Henrietta squirmed, the crowd began to take an interest. Eyes swivelled towards Alfie. He was holding in his hand what every man, woman and child desired and if he didn't get out of there fast every man, woman and child would try to take it from him. He shoved the chicken inside his jacket and ran, dodging outstretched arms that poked out of the crowd like knitting needles from a ball of

16

wool. The last thing he heard as he plunged into Hyde Park was a scream from Dr Shard that echoed through the trees.

'DON'T YOU DARE EAT IT!'

Up until then that thought had not occurred to Alfie. Now he couldn't get it out of his head. Eat the chicken? Consume the Luck Gene? Why not? He was both hungry and unlucky, which made him the perfect candidate. Why not kill two birds with one stone, so to speak?

But first he had to get away. Behind him a few gung-ho members of the crowd had started to give chase. Alfie didn't stop to count heads. In their haste to catch up with him they stampeded over the stage, trampling Dr Shard. But Alfie knew all the backstreets and alleyways and he was not going to be easy to catch . . . especially now he had the lucky chicken.

*   *   *

Back in Park Lane, while Dr Shard was peeled off the pavement and rolled onto a stretcher like a piece of puff pastry, the Prime Minister drummed her fingers on the clasp of her shiny handbag.

'Get me that microphone,' she hissed at her Minister for Good News. 'Stop those people and get me that microphone.' She had the look of a rabid dog—wild staring eyes, flecks of foam splashed across her bottom lip. In the past she had been flawless at coping with pressure, but since the onset of this election her legendary 'common touch' was sorely missing.

'Wait!' she yelled into the microphone. Her voice had the impact of a gunshot. It ricocheted around Hyde Park Corner, silenced the birds in St James's Park and turned heads in the crowd. Having created an audience she twisted the muscles in her face until her mouth looked sad. 'I have let you down,' she trembled, allowing her voice to crack with a semblance of sorrow. 'I promised you a luckier life and now I can't deliver . . . Of course pretending that she had made a mistake was just another politician's trick, so that she could put things right with her next sentence. 'But I *will!*' she cried suddenly. 'Today I make this pledge. I shall regain the Luck Gene for you, the people. Give me your vote and I will find this snotty-nosed urchin, track him down to whichever rat-hole he lives in and bring that chicken out alive.' The Minister for Good News leant forward with a word of caution.

'What if he's eaten it?' he whispered.

'And if he has already eaten it,' she continued without pausing for breath, 'I

18

will use whatever surgical techniques are considered appropriate to extract the Luck Gene from his body.'

If anyone could manipulate a crowd into doing what it didn't know it wanted to do, it was Marjorie Lentless. The people applauded and cheered like a mob at a public execution.

CHAPTER TWO

Unaware that his fate was being sealed at the very highest level of government, Alfie squeezed through a hole in a wire fence and took a breather underneath a British Rail mulberry bush. Home was still two miles away, down the railway track where nobody would dare to follow. Taking a rest was not as stupid as it seemed. He had got himself into trouble and needed a moment to unmuddle his brain.

If he ate the chicken he would undoubtedly eat the Luck Gene as well, otherwise why would Dr Shard tell him NOT to eat it? But what would happen to him if he did? Presumably he would become lucky, which would mean . . . what? If he entered a running race he would win it; if there were two juicy steaks left on a barbecue he would get the biggest one; if his aunts told him to clean the clinkers out of the fireplace, the ash-bucket would suddenly develop a hole and he wouldn't have to do it. Whichever way he looked at it, being lucky was good. So that was that—Henrietta had to be eaten. But taken home and shared with his aunts? It should have been an easy decision, because Alfie hated his aunts, but thanks to his conscience he was in two minds. On the one mind, he didn't want his aunts being lucky as well, or their luck would cancel out his. On the other mind, they *had* looked after him all his life since his mother died, even though, in the process, they'd turned him into a Household Drudge. Actually, that was *another* reason to share the chicken with them. How many times had he been told that a Household Drudge's duty was to think of the needs and wishes of his mistresses first? But that argument ignored the fact that his stomach was rumbling. He was hungry enough to eat the chicken there and then. Cook it on an open fire with a stick through its bottom. He'd have to wring its neck and pluck it, but that wouldn't be so bad. It couldn't be worse than the time he had to skin that badger to make gloves for his aunts to go ice skating in . . . Wait, what

20

was he thinking? He'd been told to bring back something 'lovely'. That was an order. To not give them some chicken would be to *disobey* them and that was not a wise place to be. After the beating, they'd make him handwash their smalls for a week. No. He had to be sensible. He would take the chicken home and cook it for all of them.

A twig snapped at the top of the embankment. A rustle of dried leaves told Alfie he was not alone. As he swung round Alfie saw a dark figure hurtling down the bank towards him. He barely had time to cry out before the man struck him with his shoulder. The chicken fell out from underneath Alfie's jacket, squawked and ran off down the track, as Alfie pitched forward and banged his forehead on a pile of loose stones.

He braced himself for a second blow, but none came. Turning his head, he discovered why. His attacker was out cold, lying with his head resting on the corner of a wooden sleeper. A drop of blood trickled down his temple and dripped through his long black hair onto the collar of his leather jacket, which was stained and smelt as though it had been soaked in essence of bad eggs. It was the man who'd been driving the yellow taxi. Why was he following Alfie? Until today their paths

21

had never crossed. Unless . . .

When Alfie had seen the man staring at the Lucky Hen in the middle of the road he had thought it was a look of terror, but maybe he'd been wrong. Perhaps it had been a look of steely determination from a chicken killer! The cab driver wasn't chasing Alfie at all. He was after Henrietta!

Alfie dragged himself to his feet, winced as he touched the lump that was starting to swell on his forehead, and set off in pursuit of the Lucky Hen, which had paused a hundred metres down the track to peck at a polystyrene box. Without warning, a rush of wind knocked Alfie flat. An angry blast of a train's horn was followed by a weight of hot, heavy metal thundering past his ear. He hadn't heard it approaching. He curled into a ball and covered his head with his hands. Seconds later, as the train disappeared around the bend Alfie opened his eyes, expecting to see chicken pate, but on the track in front of him Henrietta was still alive and pecking. The train had passed directly over her head. But then what had Alfie expected from the Luckiest Hen in the World?

*   *   *

At exactly the same moment Alfie was scooping Henrietta into his arms and heading off down the track towards home, Marjorie Lentless was standing outside the Dorchester Hotel, giving the ear of her Head of Security a right good chewing. He was a Yorkshireman; a chisel-jawed, hunky, chunky man's man, called Inspector Champion, who had been a policeman for over forty years, and in all that time had never heard the riot act read so loudly.

'If I don't have that Lucky Hen back in my hands by first thing tomorrow morning,' she yelled, 'you can consider your career over!'

'Understood,' said the hero from Halifax. 'There's no chance I'll be out-thought by a chicken, ma'am. If I don't have that fowl back here by first thing tomorrow morning you have my permission to hunt me down with dogs and stick my head on a spike outside the city gates.'

The Prime Minister grimaced. 'Thank you,' she said. 'But even I won't be taking you up on that offer.'

'If I might say so ma'am, you've missed my point,' he said. 'I only said that, because I *don't* fail, you see. Never. I'm a one-man arresting-machine! So it's a joke.'

Marjorie Lentless thought jokes were a

waste of time, a bit like reading novels and listening to music. 'Just go and get the chicken!' she snapped.

Inspector Champion saluted briskly and ran off into Hyde Park.

*   *   *

Alfie reached the end of the line and jumped down off the embankment wall into the delivery yard at the back of the local supermarket. Underneath his jacket the Lucky Hen was getting heavier by the second. At least he was nearly home. Soon he'd be off the streets and out of harm's way . . .

Except he wasn't alone.

There was somebody else in the delivery yard with him. He couldn't see anyone, but over by the dustbins, he could hear human voices howling like coyotes. A head bobbed up above the steel rim. The tangle of long, matted hair, the colour of red sand, identified its owner. His name was Fox, a feral creature who, as far as Alfie knew, lived on the common with his tribe of thieves. He was Alfie's age, but he was dangerous. Alfie had met him several times before and on each occasion had left with his pockets lighter. It amused Fox to relieve other children of their pocket

24

money. He was always polite and always explained why he was doing it, but there was something detached and frightening about him. It was the assassin's smile.

'Got a habit, see. Wouldn't do this otherwise. Some children are addicted to chocolate, some to cream cake or lemonade . . . me? It's chicken. I can't go a day without it.' Alfie knew this to be true. It was legend. Fox loved chicken, in much the same way as ogres love children. And Alfie had a chicken in his jacket.

'Oi!' It wasn't Fox who spotted Alfie, but Terry the Horse, one of Fox's tribe, with the long face and spotty chin. Out of the dustbins either side of him, popped two more heads. All three had matted dreadlocks just like Fox. There was Furball, also known as the hairy one, and Obi-Juan, so called because he knew nothing. All four of them were dressed identically in red jackets, green trousers and shiny gold buttons. It was their uniform. Alfie could see they had been rummaging for cooked chicken; their mouths were glistening with grease. But here was a new toy to play with . . . Alfie had one chance before they discovered Henrietta—run now and beat them to the gate—but before he could move Fox had jumped out of the dustbin, dashed thirty

25

yards and was standing in front of him, barring his way.

'How did you do that?' Alfie gasped.

'Hello, Master Pluck,' grinned Fox, as the rest of the tribe gathered round. 'Got any spare change? Don't care if it's only chicken feed!' As the tribe laughed at their leader's bad joke—because that's what you did when you were 'Tribe'—a real fox slid between Fox's legs and eyeballed Alfie with a fearless eye. 'You've met Wolfie,' he said as the fox crouched down and bared its teeth. 'You can stroke him if you like, but be warned he's partial to human fingers!' Fox snaggled a laugh and scratched his neck like a dog scratching fleas. Alfie noticed a small clump of hair was missing from the top of his head. 'What you staring at?' Fox's tone became aggressive. 'Never seen mange before?'

'No,' said Alfie. 'I've got to go now.' He tried to walk casually towards the gate, but Fox cut him off again.

'What have you got under there?' he said, prodding Alfie's bulge.

'Nothing,' blurted Alfie. If Fox discovered Henrietta he'd want to eat her immediately and Alfie wouldn't get a sniff of the Luck Gene.

'Then why's your stomach moving?'

Alfie couldn't think of an excuse. 'If I

said I was pregnant would you believe me?'

'Not likely,' said Fox.

'Then I ate a hamburger this morning that wasn't quite dead.' In his anxiety, Alfie clutched the Lucky Hen too tightly and she squawked.

'It's a chicken,' whooped the boy with matted dreadlocks. Fox lunged forward and ripped open the jacket, but as he did so a deep voice called out, 'Freeze!'

Fox and his tribe turned towards the noise. Alfie saw his chance and bolted. Through the gate, down the side road and into the High Street, where he took one look at the traffic speeding past in both directions and simply ran straight across.

'Please be lucky, Henrietta!' he hollered as horns blared and the bubble of luck laid a miraculous path between braking cars.

More importantly, Fox and his tribe, and the chunky chap who had tried to accost them—Inspector Champion no less—did not try to follow. This was partly because none of them wanted to die, but also because Alfie's insanity had caused a circus vehicle to jack-knife, spilling a variety of exotic creatures into the middle of the road. Fox and his tribe were far too busy chasing llamas and peacocks to be bothered with Alfie, while Inspector Champion, a policeman to his bones, felt it was his public duty to resolve the traffic crisis first before resuming his pursuit.

* * *

Alfie was home free. As he passed Chango's Chicken Shack there was a young woman leaning against the door chewing gum. She was in her early twenties and had a mane of red hair that fanned out from underneath her paper hat.

'Hello, Alfie,' she said, smiling.

'Hello, Red,' Alfie blushed. Why was Fox's big sister the only person who made him do that?

'Has Fox been giving you a hard time again?'

'No,' he said, not wanting to sound like a wimp.

'Because if he has,' she continued, 'I'll pop his head in the deep fat fryer!'

Alfie laughed. 'I can look after myself,' he said.

'Well, you ever need anything, Alfie, you come to me. Because you are now officially my number one favourite man.'

Alfie blushed again. This type of talk was embarrassing. 'Oh,' he said. 'Why's that?'

'Because of all those chickens in the road!' She pointed a long red fingernail at a truck of chicken carcasses that had overturned in the chaos behind him. 'I was only made manager of this restaurant last week and what do you do? You bring a ton of free chickens to my door. My bosses are going to love me. You're my lucky star!' And with that she plunged into the fray.

Alfie barely noticed the walk home. All he could think about was Red's beautiful hair and that effortless way she had of making him feel like he counted. If his aunts died tomorrow, choked to death by the weight of an unexpected locust swarm, for example, Alfie could think of nobody else he'd rather live with.

For the time being, however, his grisly aunts were still alive. But maybe, once he'd eaten his share of the lucky chicken that would all change.

CHAPTER THREE

13 Mire Road was a shambles of a house. Positioned at one end of a smart terrace it looked as though it was about to fall down, or at least as though the weeds in the front garden were holding it up. The wooden windows were rotten, the window panes were cracked and the front door hung at a rakish angle after a spot of subsidence.

Inside it was no better. Faded curtains hung in tatters, carpets had disintegrated into holes and the walls were wet with mould.

Alfie shoved open the front door with his shoulder and was greeted by a barrage of catcalls from the front room. 'Is that you, boy?'

'Where've you been?'

'What is the point of a Household Drudge if he's never around to drudge when you need him?!'

Alfie followed the double-barrelled howl into the sitting room where he found his only living relatives lying top to toe in a tin bath full of mud like a pair of elephant seals.

'I've been doing what you asked and getting something to eat,' he said bowing his head in what he hoped looked like a gesture of respect, but was in fact a clever way of averting his eyes from the hideous mountains of muddy flesh in front of him.

'Sock in it!' bellowed Hecate. 'That wheedling voice of yours makes the hairs stand up in my ears!'

'But you asked me to bring you something back.' Alfie pulled Henrietta out from under his jacket, causing Mohana to scream like a small girl.

'What is it?!' she wailed.

30

'A chicken,' said Alfie. Had his aunts really never seen one before?

'Liar!' snarled Hecate. 'Chicken comes wrapped in plastic not with feathers. Get that nasty dirty thing out of here.'

'So you don't want to eat it?' Alfie asked casually, trying not to let on that their loss was his lucky gain.

'Eat that?' she scoffed. 'We don't trust food that comes with a face. You never know what it's thinking.'

'Stupid question,' muttered Mohana. 'And can't you see that we are on a diet?'

All Alfie could see that they were in a bath full of mud. 'It's a very unusual diet,' he said weakly.

'It is a no-fat no-calorie no-carbohydrate no-food diet!' she snapped, 'called *Slime Yourself Thin.*'

'How does it work?' Over the years, Alfie had discovered that if he feigned an interest in his aunts' madcap schemes it made them not quite so nasty to him.

'Use your brain,' sneered Hecate. 'If we're covered in mud how can we grip the handle to open the larder door? We're not superhuman. Or hold a knife, or lick our fingers after a chocolate bar? Nobody can eat mud, can they?'

'I see,' said Alfie.

'Fathead!' jeered Mohana, flicking a

31

dollop of mud into Alfie's eye.

He took that as his cue to leave. Now would be the perfect time to get lucky.

Tingling with excitement and not a little trepidation, Alfie went into the kitchen, covered the Lucky Hen's head with a tea towel to stop it staring at him, and twisted its neck. Then he plucked it and cooked it and sucked every bone till there was not a trace of Henrietta left. Not even her brain. At the last moment, just before throwing it in the bin, Alfie had remembered Dr Shard screaming for the brain in Park Lane. Why would he have done that if it hadn't been important? He washed the brain down with a mug of sweet tea to take the taste away. Afterwards he sat at the table and prodded his tummy, thinking about the Luck Gene. Was it in there? Was it hooking its little genetic claws into his stomach wall and climbing up his veins towards his brain? Did he feel lucky? There was only one way to find out. He picked up a bone from the roasting tin, took careful aim and flicked it at a fly that had just settled on the wall. It struck the fly across the wings and knocked it into the sink.

Alfie smiled.

*   *   *

A shout from next door told Alfie that his aunts had finished dieting and wanted a pot of green tea and some Squashed-Fly biscuits immediately. For once, Alfie didn't mind dancing to their tune. After all, this was his first chance to see if his luck would hold.

He climbed onto a chair, lifted the brown tin from the shelf and took out ten biscuits, which he laid on a plate. Alfie gathered up some dead flies from the kitchen windowsill, and using the tip of a sharp knife, pushed them in between the crunchy outer layers of the biscuits until they were indistinguishable from the raisins. He trotted innocently through to the sitting room with the tray, poured the tea and, without a trace of a smirk on his face, offered the biscuits to his aunts.

'Delicious!' moaned Mohana, running her tongue around her lips to pick up the residue of crumbs.

'Divine!' roared her sister.

But Alfie's triumph was short-lived.

'Television. Quick!'

This always happened. The sisters liked their pleasures in twos and threes—boxes of chocolates, with wedding magazines, with lavender cushions, with pork scratchings, with marshmallow ice cream, with fluffy pink kittens and with *Keep*

Young and Beautiful, their favourite TV show. And it was on right now.

Alfie didn't mind blowing on their sheets before bedtime to warm them up, or even standing next to the sink while they brushed their teeth so that they could use his hair as a hand towel, but television was exhausting. The sisters were too mean to pay for electricity, which meant that Alfie had to generate it for them.

He dragged the tarpaulin off the generator in the corner of the room and pulled out the locking pin on the running wheel. He must have sighed, because the sisters turned on him like two scalded scorpions.

'What are you miserable about now, boy?'

Alfie climbed inside the wooden rat-wheel and started to run.

'I don't see why we can't have normal electricity like everyone else in the world,' he said, as the power meter registered a charge and the TV came on. The picture rolled and flickered.

'Faster!' yelled Hecate. 'It's not our fault if we haven't got enough money to pay our bills.'

'You could spend less on useless beauty products,' Alfie mumbled to himself.

'I heard that!' snarled Mohana. 'You

34

ungrateful wretch! We pluck you from the gutter after your own mother has abandoned you and this is the thanks we get!'

Why was it that every time he stood up for himself, Hecate and Mohana made him feel guilty? He didn't ask to lose his mother!

'We clothe you, we feed you, we sacrifice our lives for you and this is how you repay us.'

'Don't blame us!' snarled Hecate. 'Blame that thieving Prime Minister. She's the person who's snatched our money off us with taxes for that useless tin can moon mission of hers!'

Mohana nodded vigorously.

'Bleeding us dry so we can't pay our bills! Evil witch! Why should I eat Squashed-Fly biscuits while other people eat caviar? What's that all about then?'

'You don't like caviar,' said Hecate. 'And you *love* Squashed-Fly biscuits.'

'You know me too well,' giggled Mohana. 'And these Squashed-Fly biscuits *are* exquisitely crunchy!'

*   *   *

The News followed *Keep Young and Beautiful.* Alfie nearly fell off the rat-wheel

35

when he recognised his own face on a short clip of blurred mobile phone footage that was playing underneath the headlines, footage of a grubby boy sprinting into Hyde Park while attempting to shove a Lucky Hen underneath his jacket.

'Who's that?' barked Hecate, leaning forward and squinting at the screen. Alfie slowed to a halt so that the picture cut out.

'Nobody,' he said.

'Keep running!' yelled his aunts. 'Or we'll stuff pots and pans in your mattress.'

Alfie waited eight seconds before starting to run again, hoping that eight seconds was long enough for his face to have disappeared.

He was lucky. When the picture rolled back onto the screen, Lily Quick, the reporter who had so irritated the Prime Minister was on camera.

'This so-called Luck Gene was created by Dr Leviticus Shard who dropped thousands of eggs off a skyscraper and bred hens from the lucky ones that didn't break. To demonstrate his ground-breaking discovery he threw the Lucky Hen into the middle of the traffic on a busy Park Lane. What happened was both extraordinary and inexplicable. The hen survived. Somehow the cars avoided it. Until, that is, a yellow cab clipped it from behind and Lucky Henrietta ended up in the arms of a mystery youth.'

Without warning, they cut to the same footage of Alfie escaping. He was too slow to stop the wheel and when his startled aunts sat forward in their bath they nearly caused a mud slide.

'I recognise that chicken!' cried Hecate.

'Keep running!' shrieked Mohana as Alfie slowed. When the picture returned Lily Quick was in the middle of her dramatic final sentence and Alfie feared the worst.

'. . . has eaten the chicken the Luck Gene will almost certainly have passed into his body and if that is the case we could be looking at the creation of the luckiest boy in the world.'

The aunts stood up in amazement and, covered in nothing but cold mud, turned to face Alfie.

'Well go on then!' Mohana yelled. 'Fetch us our bit of chicken as well.'

'We want our luck!' cackled Hecate. 'Bring me a lucky drumstick!'

'But you said you didn't want any,' Alfie said, wincing.

'You've eaten it!' Hecate screamed.

'You said I should.'

'We'd lost our minds!' bellowed Mohana. 'We were faint from lack of food. You took advantage of our diet, you selfish, selfish boy!'

As his aunts stepped out of the bath their bodies dripped with mud like two chocolate fountains.

'Just think what we could have done with a wing of luck, Hecate! A husband each, a win on the lottery, two new bodies and a voluminous villa in Spain!'

'We have spoiled you, boy, and now you think only of yourself. You have callously squandered our one chance of happiness.' Hecate raised her hand and slapped Alfie hard across the cheek. 'We, who have *never* been lucky, sacrifice everything for you and what do we get in return? Thoughtlessness, greed and NO chicken!'

Still smarting from the blow, Alfie replied before he had quelled his anger.

'I think you've been very lucky,' he said. 'When I came to live with you, you got yourself a free Household Drudge.' Even as he said it he knew he'd overstepped the mark.

The aunts fell silent and the room chilled.

'I think we should eat him,' Hecate said calmly to her sister. 'I think we should wring his neck and consume him, just like he consumed the lucky chicken.'

Alfie could not tell if she was being

serious. He hoped she wasn't.

'I'm not so sure,' cautioned Mohana.

'Don't go squeamish on me, dear. Alfie eats the chicken and the Luck Gene ends up inside him. We eat Alfie and hey presto, guess who the lucky ones are all of a sudden.'

'That's not what I meant,' said Mohana. 'Human meat is stuffed with calories. Think of our diet. If we eat Alfie we'll end up as big as two houses.'

'I hadn't thought of that,' Hecate gasped. 'And of course if we ate our Household Drudge who would excavate our toe jam for us?'

'Or lick the stair carpet before we came downstairs in the morning?'

'Precisely. I think we should leave him out for the werefoxes instead, don't you?'

'I think that would be best,' agreed Mohana. 'After all there is nothing a werefox enjoys more than a naughty child.'

'Nothing at all, dear.' She looked across at Alfie to check she was scaring him. 'Plucking a child out of his own back garden, dragging him off to the common, then devouring him from the inside out . . . brain first, sucked out through his ears like a slippery oyster . . . Now that is a werefox's idea of a really good night out.'

Alfie knew what was coming next. 'You

39

can sleep in the hut with Bandit!' she said.

'And think yourself lucky,' sniggered Hecate. 'Next time we'll dump you on the common!'

CHAPTER FOUR

As a matter of fact, Alfie *did* think himself lucky.

Bandit was a three-legged boxer dog and Alfie's only friend. The sisters thought they were punishing him when they sent him outside to sleep in the dog-house, but Alfie rather liked it. Normally he spent his nights alone, locked in the cellar on a straw mattress.

Bandit was lying across Alfie's thighs playing a secret game he called 'A Full Set of Legs', in which he liked to pretend that one of Alfie's legs belonged to him. Alfie often wondered where Bandit's fourth leg had gone. He decided that his aunts had chopped it off to stop the dog from running away because, for as long as he could remember, Bandit had always lived in exactly the same spot in the garden.

Alfie had drawn a ragged curtain across the entrance of the kennel to deter any passing werefoxes, but even so, he knew this was ridiculous.

'Werefoxes are supernatural,' he told Bandit. 'They can pop in and out as they please. That curtain might give them something to wipe their chops on after they've eaten us, but that's about it.'

Bandit whimpered and covered his eyes with his paws.

'Don't be such a scaredydog! They *can* come in, but they *won't*. I thought you knew. The first time a werefox appears to a naughty child is always in their dreams and I have never had a dream about a werefox.'

Alfie shifted his head so that he could whisper his next question into the dog's ear. 'So do you think the Luck Gene's worked or not? Since I ate the chicken I'd say my life has been split about 50/50 between good and bad luck.' He grimaced. 'Actually, maybe the bad luck's winning, because I've suddenly got stomach ache. I hope it's from being greedy and gobbling my food too fast, and not from eating bad science.'

Alfie pressed his hands against his stomach and stared at a knot in the wooden ceiling while he waited for the pain to recede. He really was owed a bit of luck. He couldn't remember the last time he'd been happy. When he was living with his mother? He had no memory of her, and she was dead now anyway, but he was sure that he must have been happy when he was living with her, even though it was only for a couple of weeks before she dumped him at the bus stop, jumped on the number 154 to Croydon and sent a note to his aunts to pick him up.

Alfie and Bandit yawned at the same time, which made the boy laugh.

'We understand each other,' he said sleepily, turning over and rubbing his cheek against the dog's belly. 'We'll never leave each other, will we, Bandit? If I *do* turn out to be lucky, I hope I end up in a normal family, you know, nice people who don't just want to use me as a slave.'

As his eyes began to close, Alfie's stomach griped. He twisted onto all fours and scurried outside to find a loo, while Bandit's head dropped to the floor like a dead weight.

*   *   *

Outside, Alfie was in for a shock. As he emerged into the moonlit garden somebody switched off the lights. The bruised blue sky turned black, the stars and the moon disappeared as a dark shadow

42

enveloped Alfie's head like the shadow of the sole of a giant's stamping boot. He cried out, but there was nowhere to hide.

An elephant's bottom crashed through the fence, smashing that first, then the kennel, where Alfie had been not five seconds before.

Now *that*, thought a stunned and wide-eyed Alfie, is what I would call a lucky escape.

And so it proved for Bandit as well. The elephant's bottom landed on the exact spot where Bandit's fourth leg would have been, if he'd had one.

*   *   *

The elephant's sudden appearance in Alfie's back garden was explained a few minutes later when the circus-master turned up to reclaim it. He looked exhausted, having spent the whole day rounding up his animals after some silly boy ran across the road in front of his truck.

While the circus-master went indoors to pay his aunts for the kennel, Alfie stayed in the garden. In all the excitement his stomach ache had vanished and been replaced by a warm glow of well-being. After all, it wasn't every day an elephant *nearly* sat on your head. A shiny object nestling in the grass caught his eye. It was a penny. He picked it up.

'See a penny, pick it up, and all day long you'll have good luck.'

Alfie was rather looking forward to the next day.

CHAPTER FIVE

By force of habit, Alfie rose early to do his chores. He polished Mohana's false eye and washed the sleep out of her empty socket with a flannel soaked in boiled milk and vinegar; he cleaned Hecate's dentures with a scrubbing brush; and swept the floor under their beds where their make up from the previous day had cracked and flaked off in the night. Then he went downstairs to make them tea and toast and iron their newspapers. As he spread the *Daily Sneer* across the ironing board the headline caused his heart to skip a beat.

44

LUCKY BOY STEALS LUCKY CHICKEN

[By Entertainment Correspondent — Lily Quick]

Yesterday a mystery boy stole a lucky chicken that supposedly has the power to make Britain GREAT again. Police are without a lead, but 58-year-old Inspector Champion insisted that they would get their man. 'And chicken!' he added quickly.

This is the most valuable chicken in the world.

Officials at the Ministry of Good News are concerned that the boy might have eaten the chicken already.

'He did look a bit underfed and scrawny,' said Cecil de Blouson MP. 'Hunger can often play a big part in whether we choose to eat something or not, so my guess is that if he WAS hungry and we think he

45

might have been—then he will have eaten the chicken.'

The scientist who created the Luck Gene, Dr Leviticus Shard, suffered multiple bone fractures in a freak stampede yesterday, when rampaging spectators chased after the fleeing boy. The doctor was last night recovering in a London hospital. From his near-to-death-bed he said that if the boy had eaten the chicken the Luck Gene would have passed into his body and travelled to his brain.

'It's a real problem,' said Dr Shard. 'Unless somebody qualified, somebody like me, for example, is able to surgically recover that gene from the boy's brain as soon possible, groups of vigilantes will track the boy down, remove his brain and eat it!' Dr Shard denied that this was scarermongering and appealed for the boy to come forward. 'Only I know how to winkle out that Luck Gene without threatening the

46

boy's life,' he said.

But the government disagrees. The Prime Minister herself said last night on *News! News! News!*; 'If anybody's going to operate on that brain to reclaim the Luck Gene it's the government.'

And so begins the hunt for the Luckiest Boy in the World.

Can you help solve the mystery of this boy's identity? If you know who he is or just simply want to waste some money by having a long, pointless chat with an automated voice, call 0899 465 7312 or Text LUCKY CHICKEN THIEF along with the name of the boy.

'Eat my brain!'

Alfie was horrified at the thought, before remembering that he was Alfie Pluck, the Luckiest Boy in the World. What harm could come to him? After last night's events he was sure that before anyone could get close to his brain a slice of good luck would save him. Alfie looked out of the kitchen window and stepped back in amazement. As if in confirmation of his new-found confidence there was a tiny rainbow in the garden. It arched across the grass from fence to fence, favouring nobody with its beauty but Alfie. And it was because of this extraordinary sight that Alfie did what he did next.

'Rainbows have pots of gold at the end of them,' he said to Bandit, who was lying on the mat by the back door. 'If this isn't a sign telling me to go out there and make my fortune, I don't know what is.' He picked up one of the pieces of toast that he had already buttered for Aunt Hecate and threw it carelessly onto the floor. 'Look at that!' he exclaimed gleefully. 'It fell butter side up. Another sign. I'm going to make a phone call.'

Before Alfie knew what he was doing he had phoned the premium rate number in the *Daily Sneer* and given them the information they wanted.

'Hello,' he said bullishly. 'The boy's name is Alfie Pluck and I claim my £100,000.' The line went dead. That was strange, the woman at the other end didn't ask for his name. Alfie wondered if he'd done the right thing. How could the *Daily*

Sneer give away £100,000 if they didn't know who to give it to? He called back, but the line was now engaged. What a cast-iron fool he was. That woman would claim that it was *her* who'd cracked Alfie's identity and *she'd* get the money! Now he was worried. How long would it take them to find out where he lived? And what if he *wasn't* the Luckiest Boy in the World? What if the sitting elephant and the buttered toast were just extraordinary moments of good fortune that could have happened to anyone? Somebody was going to eat his brain! What should he do? Run? Stay put? Panic? He switched on the radio to see if his name had been released and immediately heard a familiar voice:

'Today I am here at the hospital bedside of Dr Leviticus Shard.' It was the ubiquitous Lily Quick, outspoken newspaper journalist, fearless TV reporter, and hopeless nosey parker. 'How are you feeling, Doctor?'

'Yesterday,' snapped the doctor tetchily, 'I not only had my life's work stolen and lost the chance to go down in history alongside Louis Pasteur and Fred Sanger, but on top of that I broke forty-three bones in my body when I was trampled by a mob. How do you think I feel?'

'Sore,' said Lily Quick.

'*Very* sore,' grumbled the doctor.

'So, is there anything you'd like to say to the thief?' she asked.

'Apart from, why have you ruined my life?' he snapped. 'Only this . . .' He took a deep breath to make himself sound less angry. 'Do NOT eat the chicken. Everyone thinks that good luck is good, but there is a fine line between good luck and bad, and when you reach that line your life will become unbearable. You will not be able to control the Luck Gene. Only *I*, the creator, *can.* Your life will take a thousand turns for the worse.'

'It's a bit late telling me that now!' Alfie shouted at the doctor of doom, his self-belief draining away. 'Oh fug-nuts!' he yelled, flicking the radio off. 'What have I done, Bandit?'

The interview had not ended just because Alfie had stopped listening. While he finished making his aunts' breakfasts, in Dr Shard's hospital bedroom, Lily Quick continued to ask her prickly questions.

'It strikes me as strange,' she said, 'that yesterday the Luck Gene was being hailed as the saviour of mankind—a force for good that would be sold in bottles on shop shelves throughout the world, yet today you are claiming it's dangerous. Would this change in attitude be money-related at all?

I mean, it's no secret that you stand to make millions if you recover the gene.'

'You are impertinent,' he said, 'and I am tired. I'd like you to leave now.' As is always the case, his lack of a response was an answer in itself.

Lily Quick packed up her equipment and was halfway to the door when it burst open and a man with a creased face was pushed in by two junior research scientists. He smelt rather strongly of eggs and made no attempt to get out of Lily Quick's way.

'Oi!' she barked as he shouldered past her. 'Do you mind?'

The ugly man turned to confront her with corpse-cold eyes. Unsettled, she hurried out without another word.

Still with his back to the bed, the man spoke in a gruff, whispering voice.

'You wanted to see me?' he said.

Dr Shard was covered in bandages from head to toe. There was a hole for his nose so that he could breathe, one for his mouth so that he could eat, two for his ears so that he could hear (and had somewhere to attach his glasses), and two for his eyes so that he could see. His eye-holes flickered.

'Mr Mulciber?'

'How did you find me?'

'I consider trying to run down my Lucky Hen an act of personal hostility, Mr

51

Mulciber. I would be a fool if I did not know the whereabouts of my enemies . . . And how many *yellow* cabs are there in London?'

'I wasn't trying to run the chicken down,' said Mr Mulciber. 'I was trying to get close enough to steal it. I need the Luck Gene. Life has been hard since I developed my allergy to eggs.'

'All life is hard,' hissed Dr Shard.

'I was the World Champion Boiled Egg Eater. The allergy took my talent away. AllI had left was my job driving the cab. Now I live in it. When I read about your Lucky Hen I thought it might help me start my life over.'

'That's what I was told about you,' said Dr Shard. 'I was also told that you're a ruthless man who will stop at nothing to get what he wants.'

'A reputation hard-won, doctor. To win competitions, I have eaten horse manure, platypus beak, monkey nuts and even concrete.'

Dr Shard smiled behind his bandages. 'So you're insane as well,' he said. 'Good.'

'I broke nine teeth on that paving slab,' said Mr Mulciber. 'Am I here because of what I can eat?'

'No,' said Dr Shard. 'You're here because *you* need a change of luck and *I* need a partner who can be the body to my brains.'

'You want me to drive you around?'

'Amongst other things. I need a person who can help me retrieve my cash cow.'

'Oh.' Despite the fact that his face never moved, Mr Mulciber managed to look concerned. 'I didn't realise there was a cow involved,' he said. 'I hate cows.'

'It's an expression,' said the doctor sighing. 'I was going to make my fortune from selling luck around the world, and now I can't. There is another way, however. Help me retrieve the Luck Gene, Mr Mulciber. Feed it to me, and I will become the Luckiest Man in the World, and with the power of luck I shall *yet* be able to make my fortune. Only now, half of it will be yours.'

'You're prepared to share your fortune with me if I can recover the Luck Gene?'

'How's that for a deal?'

Mr Mulciber's lips flickered into the tiniest of smiles, revealing momentarily a mouth full of steel-capped teeth.

CHAPTER SIX

'13 Mire Road?' said the Prime Minister.

Alfie's address had been published in the *London Evening Snore,* a newspaper written by the same people who produced the *Daily Sneer,* and a copy had just reached Number 10 Downing Street. 'Good work, Cecil. Maybe you *will* keep your job after all.'

The Minister for Good News who had brought the information to Marjorie Lentless's attention smiled ingratiatingly.

'That *is* good news, Prime Minister,' he said. 'I am continually grateful for the opportunity you afford me to be of service to you.'

'Don't crawl,' sneered the Prime Minister. Then with a glint in her steel-blue eyes she added; 'Stay on your toes, Cecil. Don't get too comfortable. I'm looking for somebody to head up the Ministry of Scrap Heaps.'

The Prime Minister was edgy. The opinion polls had her rated the least popular Prime Minister since Sir Horace Stackpole ate a kitten for a bet, and her beloved moon mission was not going down quite as well as expected.

Friday April 14th

SHUTTLE *RENTLESS* COMING APART AT THE SEAMS!

Is our Prime Minister a waste of Space too?

[By Science Correspondent—Tessa Tube]

The utter disaster that is the British Space Programme's attempt to put a rocket on the moon can be seen today for what it is. A vanity project created by our own Prime Minister to get herself re-elected. In order to pay for the shuttle, Marjorie Lentless's government rushed through this ill-thought-out scheme and cancelled many worthwhile projects. Plans to build over sixty new schools and thirty-three new hospitals have been shelved and the money diverted into dried-

55

food technology and urination suits.

And now another piece of kit has failed. The revolutionary sleeve being tested on this flight, which claims to be able to keep a slice of toast both hot and crispy for up to one and a half hours after cooking, has malfunctioned. The astronauts are said to be extremely disappointed. Morale is at an all-time low.

'The promise of hot toast,' said one of the astronauts via satellite phone, 'is what made me apply to be an astronaut in the first place.'

Yesterday's fiasco in Hyde Park might just have been the turning point Marjorie Lentless was looking for. All she needed was that Lucky Hen.

'I think we should face facts,' said the Minister for Honesty. Marjorie Lentless laid her hand on the man's pinstriped shoulder.

'That's why you're here, George,' she smiled. 'To speak common sense to the common man. Tell it like it is. Don't hold back.'

'Well, we are all assuming that the Lucky Hen is still alive,' he said. 'I think we should assume that it is dead—eaten, to be more precise. In which case we're not so much looking to capture, detain and . . . dissect a Lucky *Hen,* but a Lucky *Boy.* And boys, in my experience, are fewer on the ground and easier to find.' It was the way he lingered over the word 'dissect' that made his proposition so distasteful.

'Thank you, George.' The Prime Minister switched her head into decision-mode; now nothing could deflect her from her goal. 'Put out a full alert for this Alfie Pluck,' she ordered. 'Monitor all gambling establishments; betting shops, race tracks, lottery ticket outlets, anywhere a wayward young man might go to test out his luck. Leave no stone unturned. Bring him in, gentlemen. Trap him, trick him, hook him to the back of a truck and tow him in by his ankles . . . I don't care! Just find me that Luck Gene!'

Even the timid Minister for Unimportant Jobs That Nobody Else Wants To Do had to admit that when Marjorie Lentless was in full sail, she was both a magnificent and a very scary beast!

*   *   *

Unfortunately the Prime Minister's chances of picking Alfie up off the street were slim. To be picked up he would have to be seen, and to be seen he would have to be out and about, not chained to the wall of the cellar with Bandit's lead and collar.

When Alfie had taken his aunts their breakfast trays and newspapers, he had been expecting a reaction to his picture being on the front page. Having missed out on eating a piece of the Luck Gene itself, he had assumed that his aunts would eagerly claim the £100,000 reward, but instead it was the thought of losing their Household Drudge that was too much to bear. 'You can't leave this house!' Hecate squealed, spread-eagling herself against the front door. 'You'll never come back.'

'Who will squeeze my toothpaste out of the tube?' Mohana screamed hysterically. 'Who will close my eyes if there is a piece of classical music I wish to listen to on Radio 3? Who will squish all those nasty tapeworms that live in Bandit's bottom?'

At one time or another, Alfie had done all of these jobs.

'You have to stay,' Hecate snarled. 'You belong to us!'

As he sat on the cellar floor and tugged at the chain around his wrist, Alfie realised that his life had to change. His aunts would never let him go willingly. It was time to leave. The Luck Gene would go to waste if he didn't. Somehow, he had to free himself from this cellar and make good his escape. But how? He searched the gloomy space for inspiration . . . a bucket, a chair and a bowl full of rat poison.

It wasn't luck he needed, but a miracle.

Then the doorbell rang.

Alfie heard whispered voices in the hall and shuffling feet above his head as Hecate and Mohana argued about who should open the door. Normally this was Alfie's job and both were anxious that lack of practice might have taken the edge off their door opening skills.

The doorbell rang for a second time.

The arguing flared to a pitch, then stopped suddenly. The door latch clicked and Alfie heard a scream followed by the thump of a falling body.

The body, Alfie discovered later, belonged to Mohana. Having lost the War of the Door with Hecate she had opened it to find a grubby boy with long, matted hair rifling through their dustbin. He turned at the sound of the latch with Henrietta's carcass hanging from his mouth. 'Lully!' he had grinned, cheekily, offering a thigh bone to Mohana, who promptly fainted, leaving a nervous Hecate on her own to deal with this undesirable bag of boy-dirt.

'Is Alfie in?' Fox said (for it was he).

'No,' Hecate replied, grabbing an aerosol can of *DEATH TO BUGS!* off the hall table. She sprayed it directly into Fox's face, but he barely flinched. 'Go away and die!' she cried, as a fox brushed past the boy's trousers and sat down next to him like a faithful dog. Its eyes latched onto Hecate like two laser beams.

'I only want to ask Alfie out to play.'

Down in the cellar, Alfie wondered why. He wasn't Fox's friend. In fact, he was scared of him, and he knew Fox never did anything that wasn't to his own advantage. He closed his eyes and willed his Aunt Hecate to not give him up.

'No you don't,' Hecate replied. 'You've never asked him out to play before. Why today of all days?'

Alfie wasn't sure whether he should thank Hecate or the Luck Gene. Either way, he was saved.

'No reason,' Fox said defensively.

'No reason!' she scoffed, flying into a rage. 'You want to kidnap him, don't you? You want to take him away and have him for yourself. Well you can't. He's ours! Begone, ragamuffin!'

Hecate tried to push the door closed in

Fox's face, but his foot jammed it open.

'It's your old mates, Fox and Wolfie,' the boy shouted into the house. 'I know you're in there, Alfie, I can smell the chicken on you!'

Realising that politeness was getting her nowhere, Hecate unhitched the Unwanted-Callers-Cattle-Prod from the hook on the back of the door and while Fox continued to rave like a madman ('I'm going to find you, Alfie, and when I do, your luck's going to be *my* luck too!'), she gave him a high-voltage blast in the pit of his stomach.

Alfie tasted fear in the dryness of his throat. If ever he managed to escape, Fox was one person he would have to avoid.

Suddenly the cellar door flew open.

'He was filthy!' shrieked Mohana, whose hair was sticking up like a hatful of snakes. 'Did you see his head? It was crawling with lice!'

'What's wrong?' asked Alfie, as his aunts flustered around him, unlocked the padlock and released him from his chains.

'We need a bath!' screeched Hecate. 'We need a steaming hot bath with carbolic soap to scrub ourselves clean!' Mohana slapped Alfie on the arm.

'Bath! Bath!' she hollered. *'We* can't run one. We don't know how. Come on, boy! Up those stairs! Chop chop!'

61

From prison to freedom in one lucky step, and all because his aunts wanted a bath! This was the clearest evidence yet that the Luck Gene worked. Alfie considered making a run for it there and then, but decided that it would be altogether easier to wait until his aunts were taking their afternoon nap, and walk out of the house unmolested. Until that time Alfie would play the loyal Household Drudge to perfection.

*   *   *

Half an hour later, the house was much calmer. Upstairs, Hecate and Mohana were drowning Fox's lice in the hot tub, while Alfie was downstairs looking for something to scrub clean the fungal infections that had mushroomed between his aunts' toes. He was wearing pink rubber gloves, had found a washing-up brush and was just considering the suitability of an ancient tin of scouring powder, when the doorbell rang again.

After Fox's visit this morning, Alfie was cautious. He lifted up the letterbox and sneaked a look outside. It wasn't Fox. It was the back of a wheelchair. He opened the door.

'Yes?' he said. 'Can I help you?' Alfie got

quite a shock when the man turned the wheelchair round. He had never seen a person covered from head to foot in bandages before.

'Alfie Pluck?' asked the muffled voice beneath the mask. It sounded vaguely familiar, but Alfie couldn't place it and wasn't taking any chances.

'Do you want me to fetch him?' he asked cleverly.

'No,' said the expressionless face. 'Just tell him this. After Dr Shard had finally created one hundred Lucky Hens, he put them in a hen house. That same night a fox broke in and killed ninety-nine of them. The ninety-nine dead hens were the hens that had run around the coop in a panic, but the surviving hen, the one that walked through the traffic on Park Lane, had been so petrified by the fox that it remained stock still throughout the attack. As luck would have it, the fox had stigmatisms in both its eyes that prevented it from seeing static objects. Good luck for one hen was bad luck for ninety-nine others.'

Alfie had no idea why this bandaged man was telling him all this, but didn't want to hang about on the doorstep any longer than he had to, in case Fox was lurking nearby.

'Oh dear,' he said, hoping a sympathetic

tone would satisfy. 'Poor chickens. Well, thank you very much, I'm sure Alfie will be fascinated when I tell him.'

The man in the wheelchair grabbed Alfie's arm with a plastered claw.

'If Alfie only remembers one thing,' he said darkly, 'make sure it is this; when good luck dances into a room, bad luck is never far behind, swishing its bushy tail of death. Only Dr Shard has the knowledge to defeat bad luck. Alfie will perish at its hands.'

He started to laugh; not a friendly chuckle, but a full-throated explosion of villainy.

Alfie made to slam the door in the bandaged man's face, but just then a second man, with long hair and a stench of bad eggs, sprang out from his hiding place behind the porch and grabbed Alfie by the neck.

'He warned you to beware the bushy tail of death,' he yelled, 'well here I am, Alfie Pluck, wagging in your face. *Your* death! Now where's that chicken?'

Alfie suddenly realised who this madman was. The driver of the yellow cab, the one who'd lunged at him on the railway track. The cabbie pulled Alfie towards him, dragging him across the bandaged man's broken legs.

'Aaaaaaaaagh! Get offffffffffffff!'

'Bandit!'

Alfie tried to call for help, but the attacker was squeezing his throat. It didn't matter. Bandit had sensed trouble and was already on his way. Bouncing up the cellar steps, he assessed the situation in a flash and leapt up onto the wheelchair.

'Noooooooooooo!' wailed the bandaged man, as Bandit landed on his legs, clamped his teeth onto the bottom of Alfie's trousers and tugged.

The cab driver was strong, but no match for a Boxer. Neither were Alfie's trousers. With a sharp pop the button-thread snapped, the trousers flew off, and the cab driver shot backwards into a bed of thorny roses. A trouserless Alfie dodged back past the bandaged man and rushed indoors, where Bandit, his most faithful of friends, was waiting to complete his rescue.

As the bandaged man leant forward in his wheelchair and grabbed hold of the door frame, Bandit stood on his hind legs and pushed hard on the back of the door with his single front paw. The bandaged man did not have time to remove his hand and seconds later was screaming again as the door hit it and crushed his fingers.

*   *   *

65

Safely indoors, Alfie was panting with panic.

'What is happening?' he shouted at Bandit. 'One minute I'm lucky, the next I'm nearly dead. I was going to run away and now I don't know what to do. All that 'bushy tail of death' stuff. Maybe, I *won't* get lucky, maybe I'll end up dead in a gutter with my brains sucked out. If it's not Fox, it'll be that spooky cab driver or, if I'm really unlucky, a werefox!'

Alfie had discarded the rubber gloves and was pacing the hall, still without his trousers on. Bandit nuzzled the boy's hand until he stood still and calmed down. 'Staying's not an option, is it?' Alfie said after a long pause. 'Everyone knows where I live so I'm better off on the streets where I can keep moving.' Without another word Alfie grabbed a pair of shorts off the clothes horse in the kitchen, heaved Bandit over the fence at the bottom of the garden, and escaped from his life of domestic slavery.

CHAPTER SEVEN

Over the wall and into the alleyway. Shorts on. Crouch down. Stay hidden. Alfie's heart was thumping. Which way should they go? Left! Bandit had chosen. Stooping, Alfie ran to the end of the alleyway and out into Creek Street. Seconds later, with Bandit frog-hopping as quickly as he could, they rejoined Mire Road. This was the dangerous bit. They had emerged two hundred yards down the road from Hecate and Mohana's front door.

Head down. Eyes up. No sign of the bandaged man and his accomplice. Press on towards the high street where the only person who had ever offered him a helping hand was about to get a visit.

*   *   *

'Hello? Red? Anybody here?'

Alfie pushed open the door to Chango's Chicken Shack. Three empty tables covered in plastic cloths were pushed against the wall. 'Hello?' The fryers were hissing, but nobody was at home. At the rear of the shop a blue door stood ajar. It led out to the back yard, from where Alfie could now hear a rattling noise, like metal dustbin lids being handled as someone put out the rubbish. 'Come on,' he whispered, but Bandit had his eye on a tray of cooked chicken wings and wasn't budging. Alfie was on his own.

Through the open door was a store room. It was dark and rather grubby. To the left there was a walk-in refrigerator with a rusty door that stood open, revealing racks of chicken carcasses hanging like pale shirts in a wardrobe. On the wall between the fridge and the door to the yard, six butcher's knives dangled off stainless steel hooks above a wooden chopping block, stained blood-red from countless beheadings. Alfie passed through and went outside.

It was a small yard with three industrial dustbins blocking the gate to the access lane. Here too appeared to be deserted.

'Red?' To Alfie's horror, four dreadlocked heads appeared over the rims of the dustbins; Fox, Furball, Terry the Horse and Obi-Juan. Did they *live* in dustbins?

'Hello, Alfie!' grinned Fox, flies buzzing around his greasy lips. 'I was looking for you earlier. Have you come to join the feast?' In the flickering of an eye Fox leapt

68

from the dustbin and landed next to Alfie, who was petrified, frozen to the spot.

'Red's not here. She was out last night so she's catching up on some sleep. Can I help?'

Alfie was conscious Fox had placed a hand on his shoulder.

'No, you're all right,' Alfie said, trying to keep it friendly so that Fox wouldn't see the panic in his eyes. Get out of there, Alfie. Run!

But Fox had unfinished business with Alfie and stood in his way.

'I came round to your house before. Did your aunts not say?'

'No,' lied Alfie.

'I heard you ate that lucky chicken.'

Already stretched taut, Alfie's nerves snapped. He pushed past Fox and tried to run into the shop, but Fox was on him before he'd even made it to the door.

'So is it true?' he asked. 'Are you the Luckiest Boy in the World?'

Face down on the concrete with Fox sitting on his back, Alfie was terrified. What was Fox going to do? Should he lie? Tell the truth? Which was going to get him hurt the least?

'Because if you are,' continued his tormentor, 'I want a share!'

The only weapon Alfie possessed was

silence. If he could keep Fox guessing maybe an opportunity would arise for him to get away. And anyway, the truth wasn't as simple as it seemed. If Alfie really was the Luckiest Boy in the World, why, when he'd just run away from home, was Fox the first person he'd bumped into? That wasn't lucky. That was unlucky. Maybe the Luck Gene *wasn't* inside him. Maybe Alfie wouldn't have to pretend at all. Not now though. *Now* was *not* the time to be testing his luck.

'I didn't eat the chicken. The papers say I did, but I didn't.'

Fox turned Alfie over and twisted the skin on his wrist painfully.

'Now I may look like a fool . . .' he said.

'Yeah,' snorted one of the tribe. Out of nowhere, Fox darted forward and punched Terry the Horse in the throat. Alfie flinched while Obi-Juan and Furball laughed out loud.

'I'm trying to work here,' exploded Fox. 'I'm trying to make us rich, but you idiots just want to have a laugh and talk rubbish.'

'I was laughing because you were funny,' said Obi-Juan.

'No you weren't, Obi. You were laughing because that's what you think I want to hear.'

'I thought we were Tribe,' coughed Terry

the Horse, regaining his voice.

'I'm trying to discuss our future with Alfie!' howled Fox, his face now red with rage. Alfie remained on the ground, too scared to move. 'So how come I found that chicken carcass in your aunties' dustbin?'

Alfie felt the full force of Fox's glare and lied again.

'I haven't eaten the chicken.'

'We'll see,' snarled Fox. 'Hand me the bag.'

Furball stepped across the yard with a sack that twisted in his hand. 'We found this when that circus truck crashed,' Fox said, holding the sack close to Alfie's ear. 'Can you guess what's inside?'

Alfie could hear something hissing.

'Of course it might just be a harmless little grass snake,' said Fox smirking. 'But then again it could be a cobra. Are you willing to find out or do you just want to tell me the truth?'

Alfie never had to make that decision. Just as Fox was opening the sack, a lump of blue ice, jettisoned from the waste chute of a passing aeroplane, fell from the sky and smashed into the concrete next to his ear. If Alfie had been centimetres away from death, the circus cobra was not quite so fortunate. The blue ice spiked its head and the sack stopped squirming. 'That was an

71

unusually lucky escape,' Fox said suspiciously. Alfie's lie was in danger of being exposed.

'Things like that fall out of aeroplanes all the time,' he said casually, trying to disguise his growing panic. 'Listen, Fox, you've got it all wrong. How can anyone *eat* a lucky chicken? It's not possible. I mean, *being eaten* is bad luck for the thing that's being eaten, right? You see what I'm saying? If the Luck Gene only lets good things happen to the creature it's inside of, then it wouldn't have let me eat the chicken, would it? Assuming I did eat the chicken, that is . . . which I didn't.'

This was what Alfie *said*. What he was *thinking* was quite the opposite. He knew that the chicken he'd eaten *was* the Lucky Hen. Therefore it must have been the chicken's good luck for Alfie to eat it, which meant that it must have been lucky for the chicken to die! And a creature that considers itself lucky to die must really hate life. From which Alfie could only deduce one thing; that eventually the Luck Gene must turn good luck into BAD . . . But *how* bad? And when was it going to happen?

The sound of a window sliding open above their heads made the five boys look up. Red poked her tousled head out.

72

'I'm trying to get some sleep,' she groaned. 'Go away!'

'Sorry, sis,' said Fox.

'What are you doing?'

'It's Alfie,' said Fox. 'He came here to see you and when I told him you were asleep he said he'd go up anyway. I had to stop him.'

'What does he want?'

Alfie picked himself up off the ground. There was no point calling Fox a liar in front of his sister. It would just make matters worse. So he went along with the story.

'Sorry,' he called up. 'You said I could ask for your help if ever I needed it, so that's what I was doing.'

'He's eaten the Luck Gene!' shouted Fox.

'No I haven't,' denied Alfie. 'I've left home, because my aunts treat me like a slave and I've had enough. And I happened to be passing, so I thought I'd come in and ask, on the off chance, if you knew of anywhere I could stay.'

'Well you can't stay here, I'm afraid,' she said. 'Me and Fox share a room as it is. I wouldn't wish the smell of him on anybody!'

The tribe laughed, but Fox was not amused. 'Why don't you stay in the den?'

73

she said. 'If I can't sleep I sometimes spend the night up there.'

'Yeah!' Fox yelped, coming back to life with a gleam in his eye. 'The den. On the common!' He grabbed Alfie's arm. 'I'll take you there right now.'

'Wait a minute . . .' squealed Alfie. 'I might not want to go to the common.'

Not the common. Not with the werefoxes! But it seemed Alfie had no choice in the matter and no further chance of escape either. Red had shut her window, and Fox and the tribe were manhandling Alfie and Bandit through the shop and out onto the street.

*　　　*　　　*

By the time they reached the common, Fox was strutting like a peacock that had just won the Lottery. Alfie kept quiet. He knew crying out would do him no good. Fox's den was on the dark, wooded side of the common rarely visited by anyone other than dog walkers. Brambles and nettles had been encouraged to grow over the wooden structure the tribe had lashed up out of woodfall and corrugated iron; then covered in a fishing net stolen from the forecourt of a local Portuguese restaurant. They'd threaded twigs and leaves through

74

the net to act as camouflage.

From the path, if you didn't know the den was there you wouldn't see it.

Wolfie greeted Bandit with raised hackles and drawn teeth, but it was Bandit who won the day. To everyone's surprise the three-legged dog broke free of his leash and chased the four-legged fox up a tree. This was to be his final act of heroism, however. Fox issued a restraining order on Bandit. Obi-Juan hobbled his hind legs with a piece of string, and laughed when Bandit fell flat on his flat nose, trying to bite him. Bandit studied the cruel boy with a calculating eye. He knew what he knew, and when he escaped he'd remember it to fuel his revenge.

With Bandit neutralised, Alfie was tied to a tree. He tried to resist, but it was futile. There were too many hands. When he was secure, Fox sent Obi-Juan to the edge of the wood to keep watch.

'Why can't I be part of the action?' he moaned.

'Because you always go too far,' said Fox.

'I won't,' said Obi-Juan. 'I want to throw something.'

'Just keep an eye out,' ordered Fox, pointing down the path.

'Throw what things?' asked Alfie anxiously.

Fox pushed Obi-Juan in the back.

'See what you've done now, you lump. You've gone and scared him.'

If Alfie wasn't scared before, he certainly was now. 'What are you going to do to me?'

In answer to his question, Fox placed an apple on top of Alfie's head.

'Don't look so puzzled,' he said. 'You've seen William Tell, the bloke who split the apple with a crossbow bolt.'

Alfie's face drained of blood. This was going too far. He would just tell Fox that he had eaten the chicken and take the consequences. 'Oh bless,' teased Fox. 'He thinks we're going to use a crossbow.'

The tribe laughed at their leader's wit. 'Have you lost your tiny mind, Alfie? This is the twenty-first century. Where am I going to find a medieval crossbow?'

'So you're not going to shoot me?' Alfie whispered, not knowing if Fox was telling the truth or not.

'Shoot you? No.' Fox pulled a baseball bat out of the leg of his trousers. 'I'm going to use this.'

*   *   *

When Alfie had stopped screaming, Fox showed him a ball and explained what the game was all about.

'Lying,' he said. 'I don't believe you when you say you haven't eaten the Lucky Hen. I think you have. In fact I know you have. So I reckon if I strike a baseball at your head it won't hit you, because you're the Luckiest Boy in the World. Right?'

He waited for Alfie to contradict him, but Alfie couldn't speak. He was concentrating too hard on the baseball bat, trying to get the Luck Gene to make it disintegrate.

'I mean none of us can really know where this ball will end up,' continued Fox. 'It might hit you right between your eyes or it might miss altogether—what do you think?'

'Smack it!' shouted Terry the Horse.

'I was asking Alfie,' said Fox, as he counted out ten paces from the tree. 'Shall I hit it or not?'

He didn't wait for an answer. Even as Alfie's lips formed the word 'not', Fox tossed the ball over his shoulder then swivelled and whacked it straight at Alfie's face. Alfie squeaked and shut his eyes as a gust of wind caressed his nose and the ball rushed past him, missing his forehead by the width of a hair, splitting the apple in two and embedding itself in the bark above his head. 'And now . . .' yelped a gleeful

Fox, as Alfie dared to breathe again, '. . . we *know.*'

Extraordinarily, having survived near-death by baseball, Alfie felt liberated. Fear had stopped him from telling the truth, but now that he was no longer afraid . . .

'So what if I *did* eat the chicken?' he said boldly. 'The Luck Gene's inside me now. You'll have to kill me to get it out.'

'Kill you?' said Fox, wrinkling his nose with disgust. 'What sort of person do you think I am?'

'Cold-blooded,' replied Alfie, who now had the bit firmly between his teeth, 'untrustworthy and ruthless.' Surprisingly, Fox did not lose his temper. Instead, he untied Alfie from the tree.

'I don't want your brain,' he said. 'I want *you,* Alfie. *You* are my lucky prize.' He let out a whoop. 'And what do lucky prizes make?'

'Money!' shouted Furball. 'Dish dash dosh!'

CHAPTER EIGHT

The fact that Alfie's life was not in immediate danger made him feel a whole lot safer. He could speak his mind as well,

78

and Fox didn't seem to care; not even when Alfie rolled his eyes contemptuously at Fox's masterplan.

'You want me to be the tribe's lucky thief?' he sighed. 'So you're not going to kill me, but you don't mind sending me to prison.'

'At least you'll have somewhere to sleep,' sniggered Obi-Juan.

'You're missing the point,' crowed Fox.

'Which is?'

'That I am an evil genius!' Fox raised his hands above his head and bowed to an imaginary audience. 'I have just invented the perfect crime using a criminal who *can't* be caught!'

'You mean me?'

'Obviously.'

'So the plan is to send me off to do some robbing, relying on the fact that I am incredibly lucky and won't get caught.'

'Brilliant, isn't it?' grinned Fox. 'And we'll keep on doing it till I'm enormously rich.'

'You mean forever?' gasped Alfie.

'Yes, of course. There's no point in stopping while the plan's still working.' Alfie did not share Fox's enthusiasm. He had only just run away from home and here he was swapping one form of slavery for another. It would not do.

'OK,' he said, 'let's give it a whirl.'

Little did Fox and his tribe know that Alfie was dreaming up a secret, alternative plan, one that would set him free of them forever. He would do the thieving as instructed, but make sure that he *did* get arrested, because if he was arrested the police would whisk him away from the tribe. If Alfie had been lucky enough to survive Death by Baseball, surely this plan was achievable.

Fox, however, was not called Fox for nothing. He was a wily operator. 'By the way,' he said, 'just in case you were planning to run away during one of the robberies, I'll be with you, and the tribe will be hanging on to Bandit until you get back.'

*　　　*　　　*

The first robbery took place on the High Street. Feeling nervous and rather small, Alfie approached a man in broad daylight and blocked his path.

'Give me all your money,' he said.

'Sure,' said the man, taking off his shoes.

'What?' cried Alfie, his eyes popping open with surprise.

'In fact you might as well have everything I own.' The man started to strip completely, folding his clothes neatly and stacking them in Alfie's arms.

'Aren't you going to scream and call the police?' Alfie thought this was the least the man could do. 'I won't stop you.'

'I wouldn't dream of it,' said the man.

'But I'm robbing you,' shouted Alfie in disbelief. 'I deserve to be arrested and go to prison.'

'On the contrary,' said his victim, 'it is I who has been robbing the planet all my life. I've been thinking of giving it all up— living in a monastery, renouncing all my worldly possessions—and up until now I didn't have the courage to do it. You've changed all that.' He had stripped out of all of his clothes and to Alfie's amazement stood naked on the pavement. 'Thank you,' he said, walking off into the sunset.

Fox was by Alfie's side in a flash.

'What did I say?' he said. 'You can't get caught. Any money in the pockets?'

They checked three times, but could only find a packet of extra-strong mints.

Alfie was perplexed. The Luck Gene had obviously chosen this man to be his first victim, because it didn't want Alfie to go to prison. Clearly 'going to prison' was *bad* luck as far as the Luck Gene was concerned, which meant that it wouldn't let it happen. Fox was right. If every person

Alfie robbed 'didn't care' he would *never* be arrested. He decided it was time to be more brazen.

*   *   *

Next was a trip to Millionaires' Row—big houses set back off a leafy street behind electric gates with spikes on. Crouched in the garden of the biggest of the big, Alfie wasn't sure what the procedure was.

'How do I do this?' he called out to Fox, ignoring the first rule of House Breaking: *keep one's voice down.*

'Well, normally burglars sneak round the back and crawl in quietly through an open window,' whispered his companion.

'Right,' said Alfie, taking a brick out from under his coat and throwing it through a window. As the alarm went off, filling the silence with loud jagged noise, Alfie stepped inside. 'I reckon I've got about three minutes till the police get here,' he said casually.

'Well, hurry up then,' urged Fox.

'Oh, there's no rush,' said Alfie, picking up a silver picture frame to admire the craftsmanship.

On this occasion, Alfie's plan worked and he was caught red-handed. Unluckily, just as the 'nasty' policeman, PC Grimm, was pushing him into the squad car everything went pear-shaped. The 'nice' policeman, PC Angelo, came rushing out of the premises waving his arms.

'Wait!' he called excitedly. 'Look what I've just found.' He was holding a seventeenth-century French carriage clock made during the reign of Louis XIV. 'This was on the front cover of the *Antiques Gazette* last week.'

It turned out the house belonged to Tony Castegliani, well-known gangster and fine-art fence. The police had never been able to pin anything on him, because whenever they had raided his house in the past somebody had tipped him off and he'd spirited the goods away. But *this* time, Alfie's unplanned break-in had caught the gangster napping. The house was stuffed with stolen goods, enough to send Tony Castegliani down for the rest of his natural life.

'And it's all thanks to you,' said PC Angelo, unlocking Alfie's handcuffs. 'Under the circumstances I don't think we'll arrest you after all.'

PC Grimm was livid. 'But he's a thief!'

'He's right!' pleaded Alfie. 'I'm a dirty rotten thief and I'll do it again!' He was desperate not to be released. But PC Angelo believed in second chances and

Alfie was removed from the car.

By now Alfie was beginning to understand how the Luck Gene worked. It would not let anything bad happen to him, like going to jail. So even if he *wanted* to go to prison the Luck Gene wouldn't let him. It saved Alfie from himself.

He had assumed that luck would always side with the good. Wrong. A gene can only operate as programmed, and the Luck Gene was programmed to bring luck to its owner—NO MATTER WHAT THE CIRCUMSTANCES!

Alfie needed to think quickly before the policemen drove away. Up until now he had been trying to do something bad to get arrested. What if he did something good? Like what? Alfie smiled . . . like letting another human being collect the reward on his head.

'If I told you I was Alfie Pluck, would you do something then?' he asked.

PC Grimm's face lit up.

'Alfie Pluck,' he said, opening the car door and stepping back out. 'The boy who ate the lucky chicken?'

Alfie nodded.

'I knew I recognised you. That explains why I couldn't arrest you.' PC Grimm was beside himself with excitement. He grabbed Alfie's arm and pressed the button on his two way radio. 'I've got him!' he cried. 'I'VE GOT HIM AND I CLAIM MY £100,000 REWARD!'

'What *are* you on about?' said the crackly voice on the other end.

'Get me Inspector Champion. NOW!'

Now this was what Alfie Pluck liked to hear. For the first time since he'd eaten the lucky chicken, Alfie felt safe.

*   *   *

Inspector Champion was in a meeting at Downing Street with a peeved Prime Minister and her cabinet of yes men when the phone rang. He took the call with his head under the table so as not to disturb Mrs Lentless who was in the middle of a speech informing everyone in the room that if *she* went down at the General Election she would take all of *them* down with her.

'Should I lose this election,' she said, 'on the day after the poll, I have organised a *compulsory* trip for everyone in this room ... on the reserve shuttle. Having seen how reliable the main craft is I think I can safely predict that none of you will be coming back!'

'Prime Minister!' Inspector Champion's cry cut her off.

'What is it?' she snapped.

'We've found him!'

'Who?'

'Alfie Pluck.'

'Excellent,' she cried. 'Bring him in with the chicken and summon the cook. I shall eat the bird tonight. And once I am infused with the Luck Gene we can set about winning the election. Who knows, with a little bit of luck I may be able to stay in power forever.'

'I'm afraid the boy has already eaten the lucky chicken,' Inspector Champion informed her. 'What do you want me to tell the arresting officer?'

For once, Marjorie Lentless was speechless. It took her all of six seconds to gather her thoughts.

'We always knew our options,' she said briskly. 'We either found this lucky boy or lost the election. Now that we have found him, however, we face a further problem. But problems are only problems if they can't be solved, and this one can.'

She had the rapt attention of her Cabinet. 'According to scientific advice there is only one way to transfer the Luck Gene from one body to another—by eating it. Now clearly I cannot eat Alfie Pluck. If the press got wind of the fact that I was a practising cannibal, my popularity might

86

take something of a nosedive. So this is my plan. We bring Alfie back here to Number 10 Downing Street. There is a store room in the basement that I will have readied as an operating theatre. We find a surgeon who is a supporter of our cause and get him to extract Alfie's brain. We then feed Alfie's brain to another chicken, which we slaughter and feed to me. Hey presto! *I'm* lucky and *we* win the election! Is that clear?'

In the stunned silence that followed, the Minister for Honesty raised his hand.

'Is this really a scientific plan,' he asked, 'or some half-baked theory that you cooked up this morning in the shower?'

'The last one,' said the PM without a blush. 'But there should be no doubt that the only chance we have of winning this election is to get Alfie Pluck back here now so that I can eat his brain.'

*   *   *

Somehow this message found its way back down the open line between Inspector Champion and PC Grimm.

'Come along,' said PC Grimm, opening the back door to the squad car, 'the Prime Minister wants to eat your brain.' Faced with the choice of going with the police and having his brain served up to the Prime Minister, or returning to Fox and a life of crime against his will, he decided to take his chances with Fox. The trouble was, how was he going to persuade PC Grimm to give up the £100,000 reward?

As luck would have it, just then PC Grimm received a text from Lottery HQ informing him that he had just won £2.5million on the mid-week draw. He instantly forgot all about Alfie and went for a dance in a nearby fountain. When PC Angelo rushed off to save his friend, who had forgotten that he couldn't swim, Alfie was left alone on the street. He didn't need a second invitation. He slipped away into the shadows and made a bee-line for Fox, the tribe, and more importantly, Bandit.

CHAPTER NINE

Back at 13 Mire Road, Hecate and Mohana were still lying in the bath that Alfie had run for them a few hours earlier. The water was cold. Their skin had turned cuttlefish white and was as wrinkled as a turkey's wattle. Unable to do anything for themselves after years of being waited on, they were incapable of getting out of the bath without Alfie handing them their towels.

'And the mushrooms are still growing between my toes!' shivered Hecate. 'He was going to fetch something to scrub them off and now they're multiplying. Oh, Mohana, what if he's been taken by the werefoxes? If they've eaten him, how will we *ever* get out of this bath?'

'You're forgetting, dear, that werefoxes are just a piece of fiction that we made up to scare him and keep him in his place.'

'Oh yes,' said Hecate, who being the more nervous of the two sisters had a liking for hysteria. 'But wouldn't it be awful if our stories had brought the werefoxes to life?'

'You're overemotional,' said her sister.

'I'm cold,' whimpered Hecate. 'It does things to my brain.'

'Both of us are cold,' said Mohana as her teeth began to chatter and rattled her false eye out of its socket. As she scooped it out of the water and squished it back in, there was a knock at the bathroom door. 'There he is now!' she cried. 'Get in here, boy!'

But the aunts were in for a nasty shock. Two *men* entered the room. One had rose petals in his hair and was covered in scratches. The other was in a wheelchair and wound round with damp bandages.

'Get out of our bathroom!' shrieked

Hecate, covering her naked body as best she could. 'We are respectable ladies.'

'What a shame,' said Mr Mulciber, leering. 'If only I was a respectable gentleman.'

He closed the door behind him.

'Now, ladies, we need to know something very important, and if you don't tell us, we're going to torture you till you do.'

'Torture us!' the aunts cried out in alarm.

Mr Mulciber whipped out a digital camera, pointed it at the bath and took a picture.

'If you don't tell us where Alfie is,' he said. 'I shall publish this photograph in the *Daily Sneer* and post it on a dating website called *www.Walrus-Fanciers.com!*'

Mohana was shocked. Mr Mulciber was the most vulgar human being she had ever met in her life.

'If I was out of this bath,' she seethed, 'you wouldn't get away with this, you low-life scum.'

'Madam,' said Mr Mulciber, 'if you were out of that bath I wouldn't be here!'

*　　　*　　　*

When Alfie hooked up with the tribe

again, Fox wanted to know what he'd told the police.

'Everything,' said Alfie boldly. 'Who I was, what I'd done.'

'Now everyone will be looking for you.'

Alfie was not prone to sudden anger, but something inside flipped. And knowing that the Luck Gene would back him up gave him a new sense of courage.

'So what?' he said. 'I'm the lucky one, remember? And on that point, Fox, I've had enough of being pushed around by you and your clones.'

From out of nowhere, Terry the Horse stepped forward and raised his fist.

'You talk to Fox with respect!' he said, aiming a punch at Alfie's chin. But Bandit had seen the danger a fraction of a second before Horse's fist moved and despite his bindings threw himself forward to teach the boy a lesson. The hobble tripped him and made him bash into Obi-Juan's legs, who in turn bumped into Terry the Horse, who lurched forward as he threw his punch. Instead of knocking Alfie out, therefore, he floored Fox, who hit the ground like a bag of wet sand. The tribe gasped as their maverick leader dragged himself to his feet and rubbed his chin.

'Sorry,' muttered Horse fearfully.

'It's all right,' said Fox, his manner

91

unexpectedly docile. 'I probably had that coming. Alfie's right,' he told his tribe. 'If we're going to get the best out of this luck thing, we need to start treating him with a bit of respect.'

Furball laughed and turned away.

'You're not serious, are you?'

'Perfectly,' said Fox. 'Look at our choices. The only way one of us is going to get lucky without Alfie's help is by eating him and none of us wants to do that.'

He bent down and cut the string between Bandit's back legs.

'Let's call a truce,' he said, offering his hand. 'You scratch my back, I'll scratch yours.'

'OK,' said Alfie as Bandit flew past him and sank his teeth into Obi-Juan's bottom. The three-legged dog had unfinished business with his erstwhile tormentor. While Bandit made his point most painfully, Fox and Alfie shook hands.

'Come on then,' shouted Fox, setting off down a side street.

'Where are we going now?' Alfie asked.

'Well, you need to lie low for a while, and a bit of rest and recuperation never hurt no one.'

'What does that mean?' frowned Furball.

'Gambling,' said Fox. 'A bit of gambling!'

Fox took Alfie and the tribe to the dogs. The five of them sneaked into a greyhound stadium through a hole in the perimeter fence to watch an afternoon meeting for Veterans Only; that is to say old dogs who still missed the thrill of a race, but had to be in bed by five.

Fox suggested that Alfie should put the bets on, because only he was lucky enough to win, but when Alfie asked for money from the tribe nobody had any.

'Is this how it's going to work?' he said. 'I scratch your back and then I scratch your back again.'

'No,' said Fox. 'I'll do my bit when I have to. I was just hoping, seeing as you're lucky, that you'd come across some money lying on the ground.'

'Well I haven't,' said Alfie.

'Not yet,' Fox said, pushing Alfie into the crowd. 'But something will come up.'

Like what? Alfie thought; raindrops magically turning into gold coins; a letter suddenly arriving by pigeon post with a million pounds inside from the will of an unknown dead relative in British Columbia; money spiders taking over the world in the next five minutes and appointing him their leader? Not very likely, was it? He might be the Luckiest Boy in the World but he was still going to look a fool when he asked the bookies to advance him some money against his winnings. Which was exactly what happened. They all sent him packing.

'Do I look like a bank?' growled one. 'What if you don't win?'

'But I *will*,' protested Alfie, realising how stupid he sounded. He couldn't say who he was or somebody might try to nab him for the reward. Besides, eleven years old was far too young to be placing bets. The law was quite clear on this matter.

Just when he thought his luck had run out, Alfie noticed a bookie called Blind Bob operating in the murky shadows at the end of the terrace. He wore dark glasses, had a tattoo of a vampire on his neck, was leaning on a white walking stick and writing up the odds on his blackboard incredibly slowly. When Alfie first saw him he was arguing with a punter who was waving a winning ticket under his nose.

'But my dog won the last race. You owe me forty pounds,' the man was saying.

'So you say,' replied Blind Bob, 'but I've only got your word for it. I can't pay out unless I can see the winning ticket.'

'But you're blind!' shouted the man with frustration. 'You can't see anything.'

'Oh that's nice,' said Blind Bob. 'Thanks for rubbing it in. I mean, for all I know, you might be a conman trying to pull a fast one with an out of date bus ticket!'

As the punter walked away, Alfie realised how lucky he'd been to witness this exchange, because it had given him a brilliant idea.

He tore a piece of paper out of an old newspaper, trimmed it till it was about the size of a five-pound note, crumpled it up and pushed it into Blind Bob's hand.

'Five pounds on Knackered Boy in the next race, please.'

'Is this a five-pound note?' asked the blind man.

'Yes it is,' lied Alfie. The bookie pushed the piece of paper into his pocket and beckoned Alfie forward. 'How old are you?' he asked.

'Twenty-one,' said Alfie.

The bookie thrust out a hand, grabbed Alfie by the collar of his shirt and dragged him close.

'With a voice like a girl? Get lost, kid!' he snarled. 'You'll lose me my license.'

'Then give me back my five pounds,' said Alfie, putting the Luck Gene to the test. If the tattooed man gave himself away now it would prove that the luck was working in Alfie's favour, but if he didn't . . .'

'I'd give it back if it was a real one, you little thief! Now scarper before I belt you one!' Bingo! Blind Bob had showed his hand.

'*Me* the thief!' Alfie shouted in a voice so loud that everyone looked round. 'Who's pretending he's blind so that he can steal money from his punters?'

'I *am* blind,' hissed Blind Bob nervously. 'Keep your voice down.'

'In that case,' challenged Alfie. 'How come you knew it wasn't a real five pound note?'

In the crowd, a number of Blind Bob's regular customers were watching the argument closely. Blind Bob spotted them and realised in an instant that if any of them suspected him of cheating them out of their winnings, he'd be in for the hiding of his life.

'Honestly, good sir, I can't see nothing,' he said pitifully. 'But you sound like you could easily be twenty-one, so I'm prepared to believe you.'

'I am twenty-one,' said Alfie in his squeaky unbroken voice.

'And very manly tones you have too, sir.'

'Thank you,' said Alfie.

'Now Knackered Boy you said. Wise choice.'

And so it proved. It romped home by

fifteen lengths and Alfie won a bundle.

*   *   *

This was the first time Alfie had manipulated the Luck Gene to get what he wanted. It set him thinking. If he could stay in control of the Luck Gene, just imagine what he could achieve. Nothing would be impossible. He'd be a god!

That was a scary thought.

CHAPTER TEN

In Whitehall the fallout from the botched attempt to arrest Alfie was claiming scalps. The Scapegoat Minister and the Junior Minister in the Department of Only Here To Make It Look Like We're Doing Stuff had already been sacked, and Inspector Champion, as the senior officer in charge of the operation to arrest Alfie, was having his performance evaluated.

'It's not just *me* you've let down, Inspector,' screamed the Prime Minister. 'You've let down yourself, your badge, your family, your work colleagues, your friends, your teachers, your pets, the people who look after your money in the bank, the people in your local newsagent who rely on you for a cheery wink and a smile to brighten their day, the farmers who grow your food, the hospital workers where you were born, the football team you supported when you were a boy and the weather reporters who work so damn hard just to get the weather right for you! All of them are gravely disappointed.'

Inspector Champion shuffled his feet.

'What about my aunts and uncles?' he said. 'I was always close to them.'

'Especially them,' said the Prime Minister. 'And your cousins. You've failed them all, Inspector. The country has asked you to shoulder the responsibility for catching this chicken thief and you've spat in its eye.'

'I know,' he said, staring shamefacedly at the floor. 'I'm not proud of myself.'

'Nor should you be!' she screeched. 'If I was a man . . .'

'Which you nearly are,' chipped in the Minister for Honesty.

'. . . if I was a man, I'd take you outside and thrash you to within an inch of your life.'

Sucking in a breath, Inspector Champion uncurled his heroic frame and pushed back his shoulders.

'I shall not fail you a second time.' His

faltering voice was choked with emotion. 'I shall personally see to it that Alfie Pluck is brought to you, Prime Minister, dead or alive.'

'Alive would be best,' said the Minister for Good News. 'We're not in the Wild West now, Inspector.'

When the door closed and the Inspector's big boots had clomped down the staircase, Marjorie Lentless turned to her cabinet ministers and fixed them with a gimlet eye.

'You do understand why we need to find Alfie Pluck, don't you?' she said. There was a general mumbling of 'Yes, yes,' from the ministers, but it was far from convincing. 'Because,' she pressed on, irritated by their lack of commitment, 'when I eat the chicken that's eaten his brain the Luck Gene will flow through my body and will be present in every decision I take.'

The Minister for Honesty put up his hand.

'May I remind you, Prime Minister, that in Park Lane you did promise the British people luck in a bottle on every shelf of every shop in the land.'

'And your point is?'

'My point is, Prime Minister, that if you eat the whole chicken . . .'

'What do you mean IF!' she barked. 'I have to eat it all. How else can I become the luckiest person in the world?'

'But there won't be any left for your people,' he reminded her. 'We all accept that you will dispense your luck wisely for the benefit of your people, but that is not the same as sixty-four million individuals choosing to improve their lives by buying sixty-four million bottles of luck over the counter.'

'And think of the revenue we could raise if we introduced a Luck Tax,' added the Chancellor of the Exchequer persuasively.

Marjorie Lentless ran her gaze contemptuously over her ministers' faces.

'Very well,' she spat. 'When I have eaten the chicken's flesh we will make a nice nutritious soup out of the bones and bottle *that* for the people. Satisfied? The important thing is that I am lucky. After all, we want the Space Programme to be a good news story as opposed to the disaster it is at the moment, don't we?'

'I know I do,' said the Minister for Good News. 'But why stop at the Space Programme? Why not harness the Luck Gene to ensure a British winner at Wimbledon; or better weather across the whole country—sun for nine months of the year and snow for the rest so we can start a

100

skiing industry to rival the rest of Europe; or apples that grow with custard and crumble already inside them!'

'Precisely,' cheered the Prime Minister. 'That's the sort of thinking that wins elections.'

The Home Secretary, a distinguished older gentleman, who had been around the block several times, raised his hand.

'Am I alone in finding this all a bit offensive?' he asked, looking slowly round the table for flickers of support. 'Eating a boy's brain,' he said. 'It leaves rather a nasty taste in the mouth, don't you think?'

'You are either with us or against us, Home Secretary,' smiled the Prime Minister. 'When we came into politics we all knew what we were getting into. We are the sort of people who eat tough decisions for breakfast, remember? We do whatever it takes to ensure that this great country of ours, that we love so much, enjoys the benefits of a constant feelgood factor.'

There were no more protests. Eating Alfie was now official government policy.

Just then the phone rang.

'Prime Minister!' cried the Minister for Good News excitedly. 'Unusual betting activity has been detected at a greyhound track in South London. Somebody just won fifteen races in a row!'

The Prime Minister skipped across the floor like a little girl.

'Tell Inspector Champion,' she whooped. 'Immediately! Then get onto Whitehall Vintners and order some champagne. I don't know about you, ladies and gentlemen, but I feel an election victory coming on!'

*   *   *

Alfie had backed every winner from Useless Eustace to Steady Eddie. He'd bet his winnings from the first race on the second, and the second on the third, until after the fifteenth race, Alfie had earned over four hundred pounds. Alfie thought Fox would share it half and half, but the sight of all that money made him greedy.

'I could buy one hundred chickens with this!' he cried, giving Alfie fifty pounds to be going on with. 'It was my idea to come here,' he said defensively when Alfie looked less than pleased at the split.

Hmm, thought Alfie. Fox might not be his enemy any more, but he was still the same old chancer underneath.

So a little later, when Fox threw his arms around Alfie's neck and told Alfie that he wanted him to become tribe, Alfie nodded politely and quietly made his own plans.

102

He didn't think he'd hang around that long. He'd make himself a bit of money, enough to get a room somewhere, and walk away from Fox with Bandit by his side.

'Where is Bandit?' he asked, noticing all of a sudden that the boxer had vanished.

'Obi-Juan was looking after him,' said Fox. Alfie scanned the stands.

'So where's Obi-Juan?'

Fox stopped counting the twenty-pound notes and looked up.

'There!' He pointed to a figure on the other side of the grandstand walking across the terraces towards them.

'So where's Bandit?' asked Alfie with a note of panic in his voice.

'He fell in love,' smirked Obi Juan when he arrived minutes later. There was a mean, mocking tone in his voice. 'What could I do? I said he should stay to say goodbye to you, but he wouldn't hear of it. 'Talullah is the one I love now,' he said grandly, as he hopped up the ramp onto the back of the pick-up truck in the car park and disappeared into the sunset.'

Alfie was unimpressed.

'Bandit doesn't speak,' he said.

'With his eyes,' jeered. Obi-Juan. 'He told me all of this with his hang-dog eyes.'

'So where is he?' Alfie raised his voice to

103

make it clear that he wasn't messing around.

'I just told you.'

'Tell him again!' bellowed Fox.

The fact that an angry Fox had intervened on Alfie's behalf caused the swagger to drain from the other boy's face.

'I gave him away to a man with a three-legged greyhound called Talullah. I thought they'd be suited.'

'You gave him away!'

'He deserved it,' snivelled Obi-Juan. 'He bit me.'

Fox grabbed Obi-Juan by the ears and pulled his face close to his own.

'Our golden goose has just started laying golden eggs and you upset him by giving away his dog.'

'He's gone to a good home, Fox.'

'He already HAD a good home!' roared Alfie. 'ME!' The fury of being used built up inside him until he could hold it back no longer. 'I'm going after him.' Alfie leapt off down the terraces, shrugging off the arm that was placed on his shoulder by Fox.

'No. Alfie, stop . . . please.'

Terry the Horse and Furball jumped down the steps and blocked Alfie's path, allowing Fox to catch up. He sounded genuinely sorry. 'Obi-Juan's done a stupid thing. Can't we just put it behind us? We're having such a good time.'

Alfie stared at Fox with contempt.

'Bandit was my best friend,' he said. 'My *only* friend.'

'I can be your best friend instead,' said Fox hopefully. But Alfie had had enough.

'That's it,' he said. 'Do what you like to me, Fox, but I'm not coming with you any more.'

'OK. We'll find him again,' said Fox, panicking at the thought of losing his lucky charm.

'No we won't,' said Obi-Juan. 'I didn't ask the bloke where he lived.' The sound of Obi Juan's voice was an instant irritant to Fox, and spinning round, he jabbed Obi-Juan in his throat so that he couldn't speak any more.

'We don't want to know what *you* think,' snapped Fox. He turned back to Alfie all smiles and cajolement. 'We're a good team, you and me. I can help you get the money you need to live away from home. Bandit was a real good friend, and I'm sorry he's gone, but we're better off without a three-legged dog. He just slows us down when we're running away.'

'I am NOT coming with you,' said Alfie. 'I am the Luckiest Boy in the World and I can do what I want.'

Even as he was uttering these words

105

Inspector Champion pulled the rug from under Alfie's feet. The dog racing stopped and Alfie's face flashed up on every screen in the stadium.

SEEN THIS BOY?

GRAB HIM!

and £100,000 is yours.

Alfie froze with fear. People would do anything for that amount of money and there were thousands of them in the stadium. He felt like a fox that had just been scented by a pack of hounds. There were no rules. It was simply a question of survival. Fox, who was used to making split-second decisions, grabbed Alfie before anyone could spot him. He pushed Alfie through a hole in a nearby fence then slid after him.

'If they catch you, they'll tear you apart!' he said, as the tribe regrouped on the street outside. 'Follow me!'

Alfie did as he was told. If there was one place he trusted Fox's instincts over his own, it was out on the streets.

CHAPTER ELEVEN

The streets surrounding the greyhound stadium were now teeming with police. Fox led Alfie and his tribe to a safer place, a narrow alleyway off the main drag.

'Down here,' he said, sliding the lid off a manhole. One ladder later they were wading through the sewers, up to their ankles in cold, brown water.

'Travelling by Stinker is always quicker than going by road,' Fox informed Alfie. 'But stick close. It's easy to get lost down here.'

'Where are we going?' Alfie asked. A moment ago he had felt powerful; in control of the Luck Gene and looking forward to a new life with Bandit. Now Bandit was gone and the world was hunting him. Alfie couldn't focus on what to do next. It was one thing trusting the Luck Gene to expose a conman like Blind Bob, but relying on it to outwit thousands of people who were after his scalp was too big a risk to take. While Fox was keeping him safe Alfie decided he would go along with him.

Further back down the tunnel, Furball and Terry the Horse were sharing a joke.

'Here, Fox,' snorted Furball. 'Want to hear our idea?'

From the unsmiling set of Fox's mouth, Alfie guessed that Fox did not.

'You'll laugh at this,' Horse assured them. 'We put Alfie in a circus show—*The Incredible Death-Defying Alfie!*'

'We thought we could stand him under a piano,' sniggered Furball, 'and get people to pay to see it *not* land on his head.'

'Or we zip him into a dog suit with a tail,' said Horse, barely able to speak with mirth, 'and punters bet on how long he'll last in a dog fight with a real pit bull.'

'Or I could ask Alfie to get lucky and conjure up a couple of sewer-crocodiles to shut you lot up for good!'

A sharp rebuke from Fox strangled the laughter. It had not escaped Alfie's notice that Fox seemed to be falling out of love with his tribe. Why stick with this bunch of losers when he could move onwards and upwards with Alfie's luck?

For the next few minutes they walked in silence save for the splashing of their feet. Alfie's calves were growing numb with cold. Rounding a corner into a shaft of natural light, Fox stopped suddenly, waved the others away and beckoned Alfie towards a private recess in the wall.

'I'll tell you what I'm thinking,' he

whispered. 'You want out and I want money, right? You've got luck and I've got brains.'

'I had a dog and now I haven't,' Alfie reminded Fox bitterly.

'All right, don't go on about it. I'm trying to make it up to you here.'

In response to Fox's honesty, Alfie took a deep breath and tried to explain what he was feeling.

'*I was* nervous of you,' he said. 'I didn't want to be with you, but right now I'm glad I am.'

'We both know the truth, Alfie. You don't need me. You've got the luck.'

'That's what I keep telling myself,' Alfie said. 'Then my face appears in the stadium, thousands of people want my head and I don't believe it any more.'

'Maybe the Luck Gene knows something you don't,' said Fox. 'Maybe you being chased by loads of people is lucky and eventually it'll all turn out for the best.'

Alfie grunted sceptically. 'It doesn't feel lucky,' he said, as a rat climbed out of the water, took a rest on his shoe, then dived back in again. 'I want my life back, Fox. People think this Luck Gene's good news, and sometimes it is, but ever since I ate that chicken, everyone's been after me, because they want the luck for themselves.'

'People are selfish monsters,' Fox said casually.

Alfie scoffed. 'You can talk,' he said. 'You're the worst of the lot! You not only came after me, but you kidnapped me as well.'

'But I can't *keep* you, can I? I thought I could, but I can't.' Fox looked over his shoulder to check that the tribe were out of earshot. They were throwing stones at the rat. 'I've got a proposition.'

'Why do I think this is going to be a bad idea?' sighed Alfie.

'Did I ever tell you about my dream?' Fox continued. 'To make enough money so that one day I could buy myself a nice little chicken farm in Rio de Janeiro and sit in the sunshine on the verandah all day eating chicken.'

'Oh, you like chicken, do you?' Alfie said mockingly. 'I hadn't noticed.'

'There's nothing wrong with recycling food out of dustbins.'

'Not if you're a fox, no,' said Alfie.

'Exactly. That's why I'm called what I am . . . So, what do you think?'

'About the chicken farm? Expensive.'

'That's where you come in,' Fox said excitedly. 'I want a chicken farm, you want a new home where people can't find you. You could come away with me.' Alfie scrutinised the other boy's face for a sign that he was mocking him, but saw no guile. Although Fox was not the first person Alfie would choose to run away with, at least he was making an effort to be honest. But it still wasn't going to work.

'We haven't got the money,' Alfie said.

'No, but we could have.'

'And I've still got to find Bandit.'

'OK,' said Fox, who did not appear unduly bothered by Alfie's rejection. 'We split the money down the middle. I buy a farm and you buy yourself a cottage in the country.'

'What money?' interrupted Alfie.

'The money you're going to rob from the bank.'

Alfie rubbed his temples.

'How did we get round to me robbing a bank?'

'We haven't just got round to it,' said Fox. 'It was *always* my plan. The other two robberies were just warm-ups for the main event.'

'And what if I say no?'

'Why would you say no? You're going to get a place for you and your dog, and you won't have to live with those horrible aunts of yours again.'

'Assuming I can find Bandit.'

'With your luck?' scoffed Fox. 'Do me a

favour . . . of course you'll find him. Put your hand in the water.'

'What?'

Put your hand in the water,' said Fox.

'Why?'

'Just do it.' Fox grabbed Alfie's arm and pushed it into the slow-flowing stream of brown sludge.

'But it's full of poo!'

'Now take it out,' said Fox, releasing his grip. Alfie pulled his hand out with a rush. On the middle finger of his right hand something sparkled. It was a silver ring with a round pearl set in the middle.

'How did you do that?' gasped Alfie.

'I didn't do that,' said Fox. 'Blimey, Alfie, do I have to do all your thinking for you? The Luck Gene did that.'

'So you didn't know the ring was down there under the water?'

'Of course I didn't. I'm just proving that the Luck Gene works. The moment I saw that baseball miss your head, I realised how powerful this thing was. I knew I wouldn't have long to make money out of you before you realised it too. If you want to leave, I can't stop you. If you want somewhere to live with Bandit, go and get it.'

Alfie looked at the ring again. *Finding* it was incredible. The fact that it slipped itself onto his finger blew his mind. And actually, it might be quite fun robbing a bank knowing that it was all going to work out fine. So long as nobody got hurt, obviously.

'People get shot robbing banks,' Alfie said.

'Only if they've got guns,' said Fox. 'You don't need a gun, because you've got luck instead.'

'Well that's sorted then,' Alfie said flippantly. 'I walk into a crowded bank, go up to the till and say give me all of your money and don't make a scene, because I've got luck in my pocket.'

Fox appeared to have lost interest. 'Oh look,' he said with a fake note of surprise in his voice. 'We're here.' He pointed up at the manhole cover above their heads. 'Never a dull moment, is there?'

Why did Alfie get the impression that Fox was not as honest as he wanted Alfie to believe? The fact they just *happened* to have stopped underneath the manhole closest to the bank Fox wanted Alfie to rob was surely no coincidence, and convincing Alfie that robbing a bank was a *good* thing to do was clearly the work of an evil genius. Alfie wanted to trust Fox, but he couldn't help but be suspicious of him.

Alfie and the tribe climbed out of the

113

sewers into an abandoned yard that looked as though it had last been used as a distribution point for Amazonian flesh-eating plants. The skeletons of half-digested rats, mice and cockatoos lay discarded by the packing bays. Having wrung out their socks, the tribe stayed put while Fox accompanied Alfie through a maze of narrow lanes to the High Street where the bank was situated.

'Nervous?' asked Fox.

'Strangely not,' said Alfie.

Fox stopped walking. 'This is as far as I go,' he said. 'When you've finished, I'll be waiting for you in the yard. Now, you know what to do?'

'Funnily enough, *no!*' exclaimed Alfie. 'I've never robbed a bank before.'

Fox laughed then turned back down the street leaving Alfie on his own.

'Good luck!' he called over his shoulder. 'Oh no, I forgot. You don't need it, do you?'

CHAPTER TWELVE

Alfie stood outside the bank wondering what his next move should be. Bank robbers took years to meticulously plan every detail of a heist. He'd had just over five minutes. Still, what he lacked in experience, perhaps he'd make up for in luck. He rubbed the pearl on his finger, then strode forward to join the line of busy people rushing in and out of the revolving doors.

The inside of the building was brightly lit. Customers were huddled around the walls to the right and behind him. Ahead were the tills—six glass windows, six tellers, all women. One of the windows was free. Alfie waited for the first person in the queue to step forward, but nobody seemed interested in being served. Maybe the Luck Gene had created an opening for him and was showing him where to go. Alfie had thought he might get a sign of some sort; a teller leaving her post to deal with a loose blackbird in the Counting Room, for example, or a security guard leaving a door open to the vault under a sign proclaiming,

NO ENTRY FOR MEMBERS OF THE PUBLIC

Loads of cash in here that would be easy to steal

Looking furtively over his shoulder Alfie walked across to the window and pressed his face to the glass.

'Hello,' he said.

'Don't hurt me,' she whispered.

'I'm not going to hurt you,' he said. 'Is anything the matter?'

Her face was twitching with fear.

'I'll give you the money,' she sobbed, 'just stay calm!'

This was extraordinary. How did she know what he was going to say and do before he knew it himself? Obviously it was the Luck Gene weaving its magic in some way, but for the life of him Alfie could not work out how. 'I've got children!' she blurted, making less and less sense. What did children have to do with anything? She'd be taking out her handbag next and showing him photographs. Alfie decided to take control of the situation. This was *his* robbery and he was in charge.

'Have you got a bag?' he asked.

'What?' she said.

'A bag to put the money in.'

'Aren't you going to tell me not to press the alarm?' she hissed nervously.

'Are you planning to?' he asked.

'No,' she said.

'Then I don't need to ask you, do I?' said Alfie.

'Please don't get angry!' she whimpered, as she opened the till and scooped the money into a sack that she had conveniently found on the shelf under the counter.

'Before you tie that up can you tell me how much is in there?' he asked.

'£,2,786.50p,' she said as she handed him the bag. 'Unmarked, non-sequential bills.'

'Oh dear,' he said. 'I think I need more than that for a house and a chicken farm. Don't go anywhere, will you?'

Alfie stepped back into the middle of the banking hall without any concrete plan in his head. To be honest, how he had managed to get any money at all when he didn't even remember starting the robbery was a bit of a mystery. The teller had done all the work for him. Still, it was all going terribly well . .

'Erm . . . Ladies and gentlemen,' he called out. 'Can I have your attention please?'

As if on cue the bank fell silent. The buzz of conversation stopped. All eyes swivelled towards him.

'I'm terribly sorry, but I've come in here to rob you!'

'Look out! He's got a gun!' shouted one of the customers over by the cashpoint.

'No, I haven't,' replied Alfie.

His denial simply intensified the panic. Customers threw their wallets and valuables into the middle of the floor where a security guard gathered them up into a black plastic sack and pushed it into Alfie's hands. Meanwhile the other five tellers were furiously emptying their tills into sacks which they then pushed through the gaps at the bottom of their windows with cries of 'I don't want to die!' and 'Take it, take it! For the love of God please take it!'

Two minutes later, and weighed down with booty, Alfie backed out of the door. As he stepped out onto the street he heard the strangest sound. The customers and employees of the bank, the people who had just lost their possessions, had broken into spontaneous applause.

*   *   *

Alfie was pleasantly surprised at how painless the robbery had been. He had been expecting at least a small amount of resistance, but like a puppy the bank had simply rolled onto its back and opened its legs for a tummy tickle. He had no idea how much money he had in the sacks but Fox would be only too happy to count it. Above him the flop-flop of a helicopter made him look up. The police were methodically working their way from block to block. He had to get off the streets. Alfie hurried down the gloomy passageway next to the bank, retraced his steps through the lanes and ran into the abandoned yard where Fox had said he would meet him. Only Fox was not there. Nobody was there.

Alfie was confused. All Fox wanted was the money. Had he been arrested? Was this a police ambush? He flattened himself against the side wall of the loading bay and waited for something to move, a glint of sunlight off the scope of a rifle. Nothing. And why would Fox double-cross him anyway? Fox was an opportunist. Having access to the Luck Gene was the best thing ever to have happened to him. But Alfie also knew that nothing happened in *his* life without a reason any more. There was no point brooding if Fox and the tribe weren't here, Alfie could be pretty sure it was for the best. It was time to look out for himself and move on.

First he had to transfer the money out of sacks into something that was easier to carry. A suitcase on wheels would be good. A gust of wind blew several sheets of newspaper off the top of a pile of rubbish, revealing a rubber wheel beneath. The wheel belonged to a red tartan suitcase that proved sufficiently capacious to hold all of the stolen money and even had three elastic pockets for the jewellery. This Luck Gene was like having a fairy godmother sitting on his shoulder granting his every wish. Inside a zip in the suitcase's lid he found a pair of dark glasses which he slipped on. Checking up and down the street, he set off in the opposite direction to the bank, looking, for all the world, like a normal eleven-year-old Scottish boy going off on holiday.

Except he wasn't going anywhere, because he didn't have a plan. For the first time since he had run away from Hecate and Mohana, Alfie was on his own. Being held captive by Fox and his tribe had been stressful, but at least he hadn't had to decide what to do next.

It suddenly came to him.

Find Bandit.

He'd go back to the dog track and ask around for the owner of a three-legged dog called Tallulah. How many three-legged dogs called Tallulah could there be? And once he'd found his best friend, he'd take a bus to the seaside and buy a caravan in the middle of a field where nobody could find him.

Having a sense of purpose made all the difference, and despite the distant wail of police sirens, he stepped out onto the main street confident that at last he knew where he was going.

*   *   *

A yellow London cab with its orange TAXI light switched off drove past Alfie, travelling in the opposite direction at speed. Nothing unusual about that, except that two hundred metres further on it slowed, swung a U-turn in the middle of the road and came back towards him. Alfie spotted its reflection in a shop window. He couldn't make out the face of the driver, but Alfie saw that he was wearing a white, figure-hugging suit and a white balaclava. It reminded him of something, but he couldn't place it. Now the cab had slowed to a walking pace and was maintaining a position fifty yards behind him. Wasn't it a yellow cab that had hit the Lucky Hen and nearly run him over on Park Lane? That day seemed so long ago now. Alfie had done more in the last few days than he had in the rest of his life put together.

That cab was definitely tailing him.

Without looking round, Alfie quickened his pace and as soon as he could, turned off the busy street into Turner Square. It was quieter here. Half of the square had been pedestrianised and the traffic was forced around a one way system which momentarily took the cars out of sight.

Alfie didn't wait for a second chance. He ran. The handle of the suitcase twisted in his hand as he flew across a zebra crossing without looking, dashed underneath a ladder, knocked over a bicycle and rushed, panting, into the first shop he could find, slamming the door behind him.

The bell rang above his head. Blood thumped behind his eyes, which remained fixed on the road outside. Thirty seconds later, the yellow taxi cruised past. Alfie ducked his head behind the OPEN sign hanging on the glass door. Had they seen him come in? Was he safe? Was the cab even following him in the first place? Maybe it was a figment of his imagination. He wasn't imagining his panic though, nor the rapid drumming of his heart.

'Can I help you?'

The lady behind the desk coughed lightly to attract Alfie's attention.

He swung round and smiled.

'Hello,' he said brightly.

'Can I help you?' she asked again.

'Oh,' he said with evident delight. 'You're a travel agent.'

Alfie could see from the suspicious furrow in the lady's brow that this comment made her think there was something odd about him. Why had he bothered to come into her shop if he wasn't looking to do a bit of travelling? And it must have been obvious from the posters of beaches and waterfalls on the walls that she was not a butcher or a greengrocer.

Alfie smiled and, trying to make it look as if he had meant to come in all along, reached out and grabbed the nearest brochure on the stand next to him—**Fly to RIO DE JANEIRO**. He thought briefly of Fox. What were the chances of picking *that* brochure up? Incredible!

As he flicked through the pages, Alfie realised that this must be another part of the Luck Gene's mission to reshape his life for the better. Why go to the cold British seaside and live in a dingy caravan, when he could fly to South America where the sun never set, where nobody would know him and where he could live as a perfectly normal human being for the rest of his life?

Except he wouldn't be able to take Bandit on the aeroplane. He hadn't thought of that. Maybe going away for the rest of his life was a bit over-the-top. Maybe he should just go for a two-week holiday, let all the fuss die down, and then slip back into the country to liberate Bandit. Yes, that was a much better plan.

He took the brochure to the lady, whose name badge identified her as Cherie, pointed to a picture of a ranch where people were riding horses, and said, 'I'd like to go here, please.'

'So you want to be a cowboy?' she asked.

'Yes,' he said, trying not to sound like he was making it up as he went along. 'I particularly like lassoing.'

'I see,' she smiled. 'And when do you want to go?'

'Today,' he said casually. 'Now. As soon as possible really. When's the next flight?'

After Cherie had taken Alfie's details, and he'd cleverly given his name as Alfie Bandit in case she recognised Pluck, she asked for payment.

'I'm assuming you *do* have the money to pay for this,' she asked doubtfully.

'Oh yes,' said Alfie opening his tartan suitcase. Lying loose on the top, a diamond necklace and a Rolex watch nestled in thick wads of bank notes.

The lady raised both eyebrows.

'How much do you want?'

Alfie gave her enough money to pay for the flight and a two-week stay at the ranch, then, while she went into a room behind the office to print out his tickets, he sat back in his chair and closed his eyes. He was doing the right thing by disappearing for a bit. Bandit would be fine for two weeks. Besides, if he stayed in the country and had his brain eaten by some luck-digger he'd be no good to Bandit at all. He'd ask Cherie to order him a taxi to take him straight to the airport. That would be nice, and after all that he'd been through no more than he deserved. He was as good as home and dry.

It was rather nice having money. Although luck was probably better overall, because without luck he wouldn't have had the money in the first place. No. Luck was the best. Definitely. He wouldn't swap it for the world.

Alfie opened his eyes and looked across at the closed door. Where was she with those tickets? He could hear her muffled voice on the telephone. They had big steaks in South America. He couldn't wait.

CHAPTER THIRTEEN

The Prime Minister had just fired the Minister for Good News.

'Cecil,' she had said. 'You're rubbish. I haven't had a bit of good news out of you for hours.'

'That's not true,' he whimpered, 'I brought you the news that there was unusual gambling activity at that greyhound track.'

'But we didn't catch him. I hold you entirely responsible.' The Minister for Good News had a tear in his eye as he begged Marjorie Lentless for another chance.

As it happened (although she would never admit it) she was running out of people to fill all of the ridiculous posts that she had created in the last few days to help her win the election.

'Very well,' she said. 'I have just created a new department. After the sudden demise of the Ministry for Good News, I have created a Ministry for Selling Bad News As If It Was Brilliant. Would you be interested in taking that on?'

Cecil de Blouson fell to one knee and kissed his boss's hand.

'Willingly,' he sniffled.

'Just as well,' said the Minister for Honesty, 'because we've just received another report on the Shuttle *Relentless.*'

The Cabinet put their head in their hands and groaned collectively.

'I don't want to hear the news from *you,*' snarled the Prime Minister. 'News about the shuttle should be broken by the Minister for News About The Shuttle. Where is he?'

'Hiding in the loo,' said the Minister for Honesty.

'Well somebody go and get him! And while we're waiting for his report perhaps somebody could tell me what we are going to do about this scurrilous headline in *The Sunday Sneer?*'

THE SUNDAY SNEER

Sunday April 16th

PM'S SPACE MISSION IS COSTING LIVES!

[By Science Correspondent—Tessa Tube]

It was revealed today that the cost of the failed mission to put Shuttle *Relentless* on the moon has escalated to £6 billion. That's enough money to not only cure cancer, but also give every man, woman and child in the country eight new kidneys, three hearts and a liver. Marjorie Lentless is the Prime Minister who puts Stars, Mars and Meteor Shars before a fully functioning set of internal organs for the people who vote her into power. *The Sunday Sneer* says: Vote For The Other People! At least they won't kill you.

'I've got an idea,' said the newly appointed Minister for Selling Bad News As If It Was Brilliant. 'How about this? We all know that every second those astronauts spend up there in space costing the taxpayers money is another vote lost, so we order the shuttle back to Earth, BUT — and here's the clever part, Prime Minister — we tell everyone that the mission has been a great success and achieved every single one of its goals. All we have to do is be a little creative with what those goals were.'

'I can tell you what those goals were,' said the Minister for Honesty. 'To make the Prime Minister look dynamic and forward thinking; to make her look like a leader for the future.' Marjorie Lentless grabbed the Minister for Honesty by the ear.

'So the fact that on take-off the battery was flat and the starter motor failed to fire,' she yelled, 'didn't exactly get us off to a great start, did it?'

'Not exactly, Prime Minister, no.'

Her eyes were raging as the Minister for News About The Shuttle sheepishly crept into the room.

'YOU!' she snarled. 'Hiding like a big girl. Too scared to bring me bad news.'

'No,' he said, cowering, 'it's *good* news.'

The Prime Minister's face softened.

'Really?' she said.

'Well, technically,' he squirmed, 'it's good news *and* bad news, but I think the good news is better. Any preference as to which you'd like to hear first?'

The PM picked up a vase of flowers and hurled it at his head. The Minister for News About The Shuttle ducked just in time and glass exploded against the wooden panelling. 'Righty-ho,' he snivelled. 'Well the bad news is that the nose cone just fell off and damaged one of the wings, and the guidance system that we bought second-hand off the American shuttle has . . . how shall I put this? It has reached the end of its usefulness, a bit like the landing gear in fact, which refuses to open.'

The Minister for Honesty raised his hand like a schoolboy.

'Excuse me, Prime Minister, but do you still think it's a good idea to appear at the election rally tonight dressed in a space suit?'

'Don't be facetious,' she said collapsing into a chair. 'And what is the good news?'

'Well,' said the Minister for News About The Space Shuttle, 'since all the computers went down and put the thruster rockets into sleep mode, we're confident that the shuttle's going to be coming back to Earth slightly sooner than we'd expected.'

From the look on the Prime Minister's face she would gladly have throttled the Minister for News About The Space Shuttle had the door not opened at that precise moment and her Private Secretary not burst in unannounced.

'Prime Minister!' she beamed. 'I thought you'd want to hear immediately. Alfie Pluck has been found! He was trying to buy a ticket to South America and pay for it with counterfeit bank notes.'

Marjorie Lentless rose from the chair and smoothed her hair.

'Now that *is* good news,' she said. 'Has Inspector Champion been informed?'

'He's on his way to the travel agency right now,' came the reply.

'Excellent!' smiled the Prime Minister turning to face her Cabinet. 'Because I think Alfie Pluck may be the only chance we've got left.'

*   *   *

Alfie Pluck was still studying the brochure and dreaming of T-bone steaks when the travel agent reappeared and said rather nervously that printing his tickets would take a little longer.

He had no inkling that seconds later Inspector Champion was going to come crashing through the door.

And crash he did. A great, big, beefy shoulder charge that rattled the glass, shuddered the door frame and scattered the brochures over the floor. Inspector Champion stood up and brushed himself down with dignity.

'Do I look like a donkey?' he said.

Alfie was taken aback. Who was this

131

large man who had just fallen through the
door and why was he asking strange
questions?

'I beg your pardon?'

'Because I'm not a donkey. So don't
treat me like one. Are we clear on that?'

'I'm not,' Alfie said.

'I am a thoroughbred racehorse, Alfie
Pluck! The best policeman in my class.
Champion by name and Champion by
nature.'

Taking strength from the fact that he was
the Luckiest Boy in the World, Alfie dared
to meet the Inspector head on.

'Can you tell me what this is about?' he
asked.

Inspector Champion strode across the
room, picked up Alfie's suitcase, banged it
down on the desk and opened the lid. The
up-draught caused one of the bank notes
to take off and flutter through the air like a
butterfly. Inspector Champion reached out
and crushed it in his hand.

'First you steal a chicken, then you rob a
bank and now you try to buy your way to
South America where the long arm of the
law can't reach you! You think you're
untouchable, don't you?'

'Well I know it sounds big-headed,' Alfie
said, 'but yes.'

The bank raid had taught Alfie that no

132

matter how high a mountain he had to climb, if he trusted to his luck he could climb it.

Unfortunately Inspector Champion thought that Alfie was laughing at him and disrespect was one thing he would not stand for.

'You're going down, boy,' he exploded. 'Think of me as your matador of fate, because I am going to drop you like a charging bull.'

'Look,' said Alfie. 'Donkeys . . . bulls . . . thoroughbred racehorses . . . can we start again? I don't know what you're talking about. Are you a policeman?'

Inspector Champion blew a fuse.

'Yes, I'm a policeman. I'm also your worst nightmare, Alfie Pluck. You think you're so clever and superior sitting there with that Luck Gene inside you. Well let me tell you I'm not impressed. And let me tell you another thing,' he chuckled meanly, 'you think you've robbed a bank, but you haven't!'

'What's that then?' asked Alfie, pointing to the booty in the suitcase.

'Fake!' roared Inspector Champion triumphantly.

Fake! Alfie's head was spinning as he tried to keep up.

'You thought you were robbing a real

bank, but it wasn't! It was a film set. They'd hired the building for the day to film a bank robbery and when you came in and did exactly what the actor was supposed to do, they thought it was him.'

That explained why Alfie felt like he'd been expected. 'But it wasn't him, it was *me,*' said Alfie. 'Why didn't they notice the difference?'

'Because, by a small quirk of fate, you're his spitting image.' This was getting ridiculous.

'Whose spitting image?'

'David Pinkerton!' screeched Cherie, leaping from her chair with excitement. Alfie had forgotten she was there. 'From the boy-wizard Barry Botter films. I knew you looked like someone.' Alfie sat down to make sense of what he'd just been told.

'So all those people gave me the money because I looked like the actor who was meant to come in and steal it as part of a film?' He laughed. 'I told you my luck was incredible!'

'No it isn't!' barked the Inspector. 'Don't you see, the bank raid failed, because the money you stole wasn't real. It was all props.'

'Which is why I rang the police,' said Cherie.

'And that's why you've been caught,'

crowed the policeman. 'It's not good luck you've got working for you, it's *bad* luck, and that makes me a very happy man indeed!'

'I beg to differ,' said Alfie. 'If you think about it, Inspector, you've come here today to arrest me for robbing a bank, but now you can't, because I've haven't. All I've done is appear in a film and stolen a few props. That's *good* luck, isn't it?'

The left-hand corner of the Inspector's mouth started to twitch.

'Oh I can arrest you,' he squeaked. 'I can definitely arrest you whether you've done anything wrong or not!'

'Under normal circumstances of course you could,' said Alfie. 'You're three times my size. If you decided to march me off to the station I wouldn't be able to stop you. But what I'm trying to tell you is that I'm NOT normal and you won't be able to do it.'

'Wrong! I am the law, Alfie Pluck. I am here to do the Prime Minister's bidding!'

'And I'm the Luckiest Boy in the World, Inspector. If you try to arrest me, something will happen to stop you.'

Of *that* Alfie had never been so sure in his life.

And he was right.

As Inspector Champion removed the

handcuffs from his back pocket and grabbed Alfie's wrists, a yellow taxi crashed through the glass window at the front of the shop, crushing a cheap aluminium desk and propelling a paperweight across the room like a rocket-launched grenade. It struck Inspector Champion on the chin and knocked him into La-La Land, as a long-haired figure wearing a leather jacket leapt out of the taxi and made straight for Alfie.

This was not quite the lucky rescue package Alfie had envisaged. As he was dragged into the back of the cab he recognised the long-haired man as the driver who had nearly run him down in Park Lane and had then turned up on his doorstep to accost him.

So he *had* been followed.

A sense of dread returned to the pit of Alfie's stomach as he was thrown down onto a hard floor. With the smell of bad eggs clinging to his nostrils, the cab reversed out through the shop front, causing it to collapse in a cloud of dust.

CHAPTER FOURTEEN

Imagine Alfie's surprise as he looked up from the floor of the cab, when who should he see huddled on the back seat, but Fox's tribe. All three of them were crying.

'Where's Fox?' Alfie asked, confused.

None of them replied, instead they indicated with frightened eyes for Alfie to look behind him. He didn't have to turn to know who was there. That bad smell gave him away.

'Well, if it isn't the boy who got me all cut up in those roses,' leered the hard, scarred face of the Park Lane cab driver, flashing his silver capped teeth. 'We've never been properly introduced. The name's Mr Mulciber.'

Behind him the cab was being driven erratically by the man in the bandages.

Mr Mulciber twisted Alfie's face towards him. 'We've been dying to see you again, Alfie Pluck. Now it's your turn to die for us!'

He sniggered lazily as he shoved Alfie back to the floor with the heel of his boot then rested his foot on the back of the boy's head, squashing his mouth closed.

There was no doubt in Alfie's mind that these men were after the Luck Gene. The doubt arose when Alfie wondered just how the Luck Gene was going to get him out of this particular mess.

Mr Mulciber was toying with the tribe. 'What am I going to do with you lot now that I've got Alfie?' he mused. 'Because I hate to be the one to tell you this, but *he's* all I want.'

'But you said you'd let us go if we helped you find him,' whimpered Terry the Horse.

'And it was *me* who spotted him on the pavement,' pleaded Obi-Juan.

'Yeah, but it was *me*,' shouted Furball, 'who saw him go into that shop.'

Alfie could not see any faces, but he could feel the panic rising.

'You don't have to get rid of us. You could take us with you,' begged Furball. 'Wherever you're going. We could help you.'

'Help us do what?' asked Mr Mulciber.

'Whatever it is you've got to do,' cried Terry the Horse desperately.

'You know something, lads, that might be a good idea,' said Mr Mulciber. 'Me and my friend in the bandages are going to a hospital called St Flukes. You might have heard of it. It was closed down last year thanks to our wonderful Prime Minister. It means that there aren't any doctors or nurses there. A bit of help might come in handy. I'll tell you what we *do* need . . .'

'What?' blurted the three boys together. 'We'll do it!'

'We need a brain surgeon,' said Mr Mulciber. 'Are any of you trained in brain surgery—you know, splitting opening a skull and cutting out the brain?'

'Brain surgery!' yelped Alfie, wrenching his face off the floor. Mr Mulciber kicked down with his heel, knocking the words out of Alfie's mouth. His manner was suddenly aggressive.

'Dream on, boys,' he said, opening the back door. 'It's the end of the road for you.'

Mr Mulciber leant across the seat and grabbed Furball.

'You could just drop us at the cinema,' Furball pleaded as he was shoved out of the moving cab.

'Or the park!' yelled Terry the Horse as he followed his mate onto the tarmac. 'We didn't see your faces!'

'OUT!' snarled Mr Mulciber at the one remaining boy. Obi-Juan did not wait to be asked twice and willingly jumped.

Mr Mulciber slammed the door behind the tribe and shut out the screaming.

'Right,' he said to Alfie. 'Now to see

what you've got inside that little head of yours!'

As Mr Mulciber bent towards him, Alfie was sure that this egg-breathed lunatic was going to slice off the top of his head and poke around in his brain there and then. This is where it ends, Alfie thought.

*   *   *

Inspector Champion shook the dust out of his hair and stood up. Glass crunched underfoot as he staggered towards the jagged hole in the shop front. Shielding his eyes from the low sun, he stepped onto the pavement and started to walk towards the main road. His eyes were still adjusting to the bright light when three boys came running down the street. Their hands and faces were bloody and grazed, and their red and green clothes were torn. Inspector Champion spread his arms wide and stopped them in their tracks.

'What are you three tykes running away from?' he growled in a manner so gruff that the frightened children told him everything . . . about the bandaged driver, the man who smelt of bad eggs, the yellow taxi, Fox, Alfie, the lot.

Maybe this was the piece of good luck that would save Inspector Champion's bacon. 'You're coming with me,' he said, marching the three boys to the nearest police station, where, in a startling coincidence to end all startling coincidences, the Desk Sergeant had his hands full with two large ladies dressed head to toe in pink.

*   *   *

Hecate was weeping her way through a box of tissues that the Desk Sergeant kept under his desk for just such emergencies. He was a kindly man who knew the value of a good nose-blow after a dog had been run over or a handbag had been snatched.

'If you could stop crying for just a second, maybe I'll be able to understand what you're saying,' he said, his pencil poised over the Crime Book.

'We've come to report a missing slave!' howled Hecate. The Desk Sergeant hesitated.

'You mean person?' he said.

'Is that what they're called now?' she replied. 'You see, we didn't get out of the bath for four and a half hours, because he wasn't there to hand us our towels.'

'That must have been very cold,' observed the Desk Sergeant, trying desperately not to imagine these two ladies in the bath. The image he had, however, of hippopotami with shower caps on refused to go away.

As the calmer of the two sisters, Mohana took control.

'We'd also like to complain about the two men in our bathroom,' she said. 'Write that down in your report, please. It was both terrifying and humiliating. There we were, as naked as the day we were born . . .' The Desk Sergeant was thinking about hippopotami again . . . and they tortured us with a camera to make us tell them where Alfie was. We didn't know, so they took *more* photographs, and only when we got out of the bath and tried to kiss them with a view to marriage did they run away.'

'Have you got a picture?' he asked.

Mohana gasped and slapped the Desk Sergeant across the face.

'How dare you,' she gasped indignantly. 'You men are all the same. Can't two ladies even take a bath nowadays without every man in a twelve-mile radius trying to sneak a peek?'

'Not a photograph of *you*,' he protested. 'A photo of your . . . I don't know what to call him . . . son, nephew, step-son?'

'Household Drudge,' sniffed Hecate.

'Him then,' said the Desk Sergeant.

Mohana produced from her pocket a

scrap of paper torn from the *Daily Sneer.*

'Of course we have a photograph,' she told the policeman. 'What do you take us for?'

It was the fuzzy still of Alfie escaping into Hyde Park with the Lucky Hen tucked under his arm.

The Desk Sergeant raised an eyebrow. 'So his name's Alfie Pluck is it?'

'Why do you say it like that?' asked Hecate. 'You make him sound like a criminal.'

'Because your little Alfie is wanted for robbery, resisting arrest, conspiracy and fraud. Not only that, but the Prime Minister herself has personally requested his immediate detention. This may come as something of a shock, ladies, but half the world is after him.'

*   *   *

Half the world might well have been after Alfie, but half the world would have to wait, because, for the time being, two men *had* him. In a deserted hospital that echoed to the flapping of wings and the billing and cooing of roosting pigeons, Alfie was strapped to a chair in a well-lit operating theatre.

Behind him, Mr Mulciber was boiling a

pan of water on a camping stove. Immersed in the water was a strange instrument that looked like an electric whisk with a long pencil probe on the end of a length of wire.

Mr Mulciber took the water off the heat, placed the instrument in a kidney bowl, handed it to the bandaged man, and then returned to his recipe for brain ragout. He placed a frying pan on the camping stove, added some groundnut oil and threw in a finely chopped onion, some garlic, two carrots, a tin of chopped tomatoes and some fresh parsley. Then he turned down the heat to let it simmer, took two plates out of a carrier bag and placed a knife and a fork on the rim of each.

'Just waiting for the meat now,' he announced.

'Excellent,' replied the bandaged man, who was wearing a green surgical gown, but struggling to pull the rubber gloves over his bandaged fingers.

'I don't mind if you can't do it today,' joked Alfie, whose relaxed approach to danger was being severely tested. The ability of the Luck Gene to get him out of tight spots had been proven time and time again. Why shouldn't it work its magic again? The trouble was, a small part of him refused to believe that the Luck Gene

144

could go on forever. Like everything edible it must have a sell-by date, and what if *this* was it? Alfie had started to scare himself. Was preventing brain surgery beyond the reaches of luck? If it was, he needed to do whatever he could to delay the operation and give the Luck Gene as long as possible to come up with a rescue plan.

'Hello,' he said conversationally. 'Have we met?'

'Don't you recognise me?' asked the man in the bandages, who had now succeeded in pulling on the gloves and was wheeling a trolley full of nasty sharp instruments towards Alfie's chair.

Alfie tried not to look. 'It's rather hard to recognise a person without a face,' he said.

'You stole my Lucky Hen,' said the bandaged man in a calm and somehow sinister tone.

'Dr Shard?' gasped Alhe.

'Don't pretend you didn't know.'

'I didn't,' he said, wondering if his heart was thumping loud enough for everyone to hear.

He knew he needed to ignore it and keep the doctor's mind off the operation. 'Anyway, it's nice to meet you after all this time. Well done with the Luck Gene, by the way. You did a great job.'

'I know,' said the doctor. 'That is why I intend to get it back.'

Alfie forced an unconvincing laugh. 'That's not going to be easy is it?'

'Shall I shut that mouth permanently?' interrupted Mr Mulciber, raising his fist above Alfie's face.

'That won't be necessary,' said Dr Shard. 'It's important Alfie knows what's going to happen to him. He made me suffer. Now it's his turn.'

He picked up a scalpel and tested its sharpness by splitting a hair in his nose. 'I shall be removing your brain, Alfie, using a new technique called Earhole Surgery.'

Alfie gulped loudly as the saliva dried in his throat.

'It was lucky, really,' continued the doctor, 'because when Mr Mulciber came across this deserted hospital he discovered that it still had electricity.'

He picked the whisk-like instrument out of the boiling water. 'I shall be using this high-speed oscillating probe to remove your brain through your ear. It's a bit like pulling a postman through a letterbox. Then Mr Mulciber will serve it up with a rich chilli sauce and I shall eat it!'

'Oh no!' cried Mr Mulciber suddenly. 'I forgot the chilli!'

'Oh dear,' quipped Dr Shard. 'That's

dinner cancelled then.'

For a brief moment Alfie believed him. He thought that the absence of chillies was the slice of luck he'd been waiting for. But Dr Shard was only joking. 'I prefer brain without chilli,' he said.

Alfie could feel hot breath on his face as the doctor leant down and whispered, 'The simple fact is, Alfie Pluck, that you ate my Lucky Hen, and wrecked my life, and now I am going to wreck *your* life for ever!'

Alfie started to squirm on the chair. Where was the luck? It should be riding over the hill right now like the US cavalry. Had it run out? Had he sneezed it out by accident? Maybe he should tell Dr Shard.

'I don't feel lucky!' he screamed. 'That means it's left my brain so there's no point cutting it out, because it's not there any more.'

'Oh it's there,' said Dr Shard. 'It never leaves of its own accord.'

'Then it's turned bad,' shouted Alfie in desperation. 'It's infected with a disease of some sort.'

'Then I shall cure it,' said Dr Shard. 'Are we ready, Mr Mulciber?'

'Nooooooo!' wailed Alfie. 'I'm sorry.'

'Too late,' said Dr Shard.

'I only ate the chicken because I was hungry!'

147

'And so am I,' said the doctor. 'Hungry for revenge!' He smiled an evil smile that nobody could see behind the bandages.

But Alfie could feel it.

CHAPTER FIFTEEN

Back at the police station, the aunts were still coming to terms with Alfie's infamy, when out of an interview room who should emerge but Fox.

After leaving Alfie in front of the bank, Fox had returned to the deserted yard to find his tribe, only to discover that they had disappeared. As he climbed a drainpipe to look for them, a police car containing none other than PCs Angelo and Grimm happened to pass by, and, spotting a long-haired, scabby-faced boy acting suspiciously, they had pulled him in for questioning. Hearing of her brother's arrest, Red had closed Chango's Chicken Shack and rushed down to the station to vouch for her brother's character, arriving just in time to stop PC Grimm from fixing Fox up with the robbery on Millionaires' Row.

Now, thanks to PC Angelo's common sense intervention, Fox was being released.

As he stepped into the foyer, followed by Red, PC Angelo and a furious PC Grimm, Hecate stopped crying and let out a scream.

'I know him!' she yelled.

The Desk Sergeant put his head into his hands and longed for the end of his shift.

'I've seen him rifling through our dustbins for old chicken bones. Arrest him!'

PC Grimm was keen to detain Fox again, but PC Angelo held firm.

'We've just let him go,' he said. 'There's no evidence he's done anything.'

'But he was sneaking around outside our house,' said Mohana. 'Ask him if he was trying to steal our Alfie.'

'You don't own him,' interjected Red. 'Alfie can live where he chooses.'

'He wants to live with us!' shouted the aunts together.

'That's not what he told me,' said Red. 'He said he was running away and asked if I knew anywhere he could live.'

'Lies!' spat Mohana. 'Arrest her too!'

'And now that I've seen what he was running away *from,* I'm ashamed that I didn't tell him to come and stay with us.'

Mohana lunged at Red only to be restrained by PC Angelo.

'This isn't helping Alfie,' he said. 'He

needs to be found.'

'And I intend to find him,' declared Red.

'Over our dead bodies!' snarled Mohana, rounding on the Desk Sergeant with a volley of contempt. 'If you can't help us find our slave then we shall have to do it ourselves. Come, Hecate, let's go.'

'We'll race you,' taunted Fox. 'Finders keepers, losers weepers!'

As Fox and Red turned to get the search under way, their route was barred by Inspector Champion, who was walking through the station door with a sorry-looking tribe in tow.

'And you're sure that's what you heard the smelly egg-man say?' he was asking. 'That they were taking Alfie to a local hospital that was closed down by the Prime Minister last year?'

'That's what he said,' said Furball. 'Just before he chucked us out the cab.'

'That'll be St Flukes,' said the Desk Sergeant. 'It was closed down to pay for her ridiculous space shuttle.'

'So that's where we'll find Alfie!' shouted four voices at the same time—Mohana and Hecate, Fox and Red.

'Not so much of the 'we'!' bellowed Inspector Champion. 'Some of us are trained to deal with situations like this. Some of us came top of the class in fact.

None of you lot are qualified to look for Alfie. You'll just get in the way. If we are to extract Alfie from this situation unharmed we have to approach this search like pros. Sergeant, get me a fast helicopter now—all the bells and whistles, and preferably bright red. You lot,' he pointed to the tribe, 'and that includes Bonnie and Clyde here, can wait in the cells . . . Oi! Do you mind? I haven't finished yet.'

Bonnie and Clyde, alias Red and Fox, had made a run for it while Inspector Champion was still talking.

'Look what you've done now!' shrieked Mohana, slapping the Inspector's shoulder. 'You've let the other team get a head start! You can't let those animals reach Alfie first!'

'Where's that helicopter?' yelled Hecate, shaking the Desk Sergeant's shoulders. 'Alfie's ours!'

*   *   *

Outside, Fox pushed Red down the manhole, followed her in and slid the lid back into position over their heads.

'What about the tribe?' she asked as they climbed down the ladder into the sewers.

'I thought they were your friends.'

'They're not family,' said Fox. 'They're

151

not like you and me. They'll only hold us back. And do you really want to share Alfie when we find him? I think we deserve a bit of luck, Red.'

His sister smiled.

'You're a cunning one, aren't you?' she said, as the water rose to her knees.

*　　　*　　　*

'Help!' Alfie's voice filled the empty corridors and rattled the useless doors of the deserted hospital. 'HELP!'

'And what exactly do you think that is going to achieve?' asked Mr Mulciber grinning despotically.

'I'm going to get lucky,' said the boy in desperation. 'Someone will hear me and rush to my rescue. HEEEEEEEEEEEEELP!'

Dr Shard looked at Mr Mulciber as if to say 'poor, deluded child', then both of them burst out laughing.

'Will you tell him or shall I?' he asked.

'Oh, do please let it be me,' jeered the ugly mug with the metal teeth. 'The only rushing being done in here, Alfie, will be when the rats rush to feast on your fresh cadaver.'

'We chose this place to nullify the Luck Gene,' added the doctor triumphantly.

'Nothing lives here, Alfie, and nothing can get in to save you!'

This was the moment that Alfie knew he really was out of luck. For whatever reason, the Luck Gene had abandoned him to the sick fantasies of a mad scientist and his stinking accomplice. Panic engulfed him. His heart thumped and his breathing came fast and shallow as he tried to wrench his arms and legs out of the straps that held them. Why had it abandoned him? Where could it have gone?

Dr Shard pressed the button on the side of the high-speed oscillating ear probe. At least, thought Alfie, his life had not been entirely miserable. He had known some luck before he died. The probe whizzed into life, screaming like an angry wasp skewered on the tip of a dentist's drill.

Now then,' cackled Dr Shard, pushing the probe towards Alfie's ear, 'don't be surprised if this sounds a little loud.'

This was it. Alfie shut his eyes. If something incredibly lucky didn't happen in the next three seconds, he was going to have his brain removed!

*   *   *

Two seconds later, the doomed British space ship, Shuttle *Relentless,* crash-landed on top of the O2 Arena on the bank of the River Thames. Its trail of debris took out fifteen of London's power stations. In the blink of an eye, the capital was thrown into darkness, and the high-speed oscillating ear probe stopped millimetres away from Alfie's ear drum.

CHAPTER SIXTEEN

Alfie opened his eyes to discover that the equipment had failed, and the operating theatre had been plunged into darkness.

'I don't believe it!' yelled Dr Shard. 'What's happened?'

The light source was limited to the dancing blue flame of the camping gas stove over which Mr Mulciber's ragout gently simmered.

'I can't operate in these conditions. Find me some light. Get me some power to this probe now!'

Mr Mulciber's eyes were still adjusting to the purple haze as he staggered towards the door, bashing his knee on an oxygen cylinder and splitting open his forehead on the corner of an empty swab cupboard.

Alfie took heart from the blackout. Granted, he didn't know what had caused it, but he *did* know that its timing was perfect. Clearly the Luck Gene had not given up on him yet.

Just then a brilliant white light flashed across the window and blinded him temporarily. It formed a circular halo on the floor, then skittered up the wall and was sucked back the way it had come. The noise of spinning rotor blades identified its source as the spotlight on a police helicopter, which Alfie judged to be hovering over the hospital.

'MULCIBER!' Dr Shard burst a blood vessel in the tip of his nose screaming for his partner in crime. 'GET ME THAT POWER ON NOW!'

*   *   *

Up in the helicopter, an agitated Inspector Champion was sharing his seat with two fat ladies. He felt like the ham in a ham sandwich. It was illegal for the police to take civilian passengers, but the Desk Sergeant had put his truncheon against his own head and told the Inspector that if he didn't remove these batty old fruitcakes from his station immediately, he would bash his own brains out. Hecate had just spotted the roof of the yellow cab parked under a tree.

'There he is!' she screamed, reaching across the Inspector to point out of the window. 'Get us down there now. Quickly! Quickly! Dive! Dive! Dive!'

'This is a helicopter not a submarine,' Inspector Champion snapped, pushing her away.

'We'll lose him to that fox-boy!' shouted Mohana, leaning over the pilot's seat and shoving the joystick forward. 'Just put it down and park it.'

'It isn't a bus either!' The Inspector grabbed her by the scruff of the neck and yanked her back into her seat. 'We can't just stop it anywhere we like. It has to be 'parked', as you call it, in an area that's wider than the rotor blades otherwise they tend to snap off. So sit down, close your squawking beaks and let the pilot do his job.'

Inspector Champion was losing patience. Three times Alfie Pluck had avoided arrest. That was three times more than any villain had ever done before. For the first time in his distinguished career Inspector Champion was staring down the twin barrels of failure and ignominy. 'What I wouldn't give right now,' he declared grimly, 'for even the tiniest slice of that Luck Gene!'

Meanwhile 'that fox-boy' was lost in the sewers.

'I thought you said you knew these Stinkers like the back of your hand,' said Red, as they stopped at their second cross-tunnels in as many minutes.

'I did,' replied Fox. 'But the back of my hand got hairy. I haven't seen it for a year.'

Red grabbed his hand and turned it over to see if he was joking. He wasn't. It was covered in a fine down of red hair.

'Give me a moment,' said Fox, closing his eyes. 'The bank was east, the police station was west and we should be travelling south. It's that tunnel there.' He pointed to the one behind Red.

'If you're wrong,' she said, 'they'll get to Alfie first.'

'We may still have a couple of miles to go,' said Fox, 'and they may have a bright red helicopter, but we can run faster than any policeman.'

Red smiled.

'Right,' she said. 'Last one at the hospital's a sissy!' And she took off, the soles of her trainers kissing the top of the water like a supersonic lizard.

*   *   *

All of Mr Mulciber's power-generating ideas were proving impractical. The hospital windows were too dirty for solar power and although the walls were running with damp, the flow was woefully inadequate for hydro-electricity. His only option, therefore, were the dead batteries in an abandoned heart defibrillator. It turned out they weren't *quite* dead. They were still tingly to the tongue. Once he'd wired them up to the probe, however, it wasn't so much *high-speed* any more as *slow-speed* . . . even *slow-and-really-painful-speed.* Imagine having your brain extracted through your ear by a drill that rotated no faster than a scooping spoon. For poor old Alfie this was *all* he could imagine, and it was terrifying. He had survived one attempt on his life, but how on earth was he going to survive two?

'FREEZE!'

The glass door to the operating theatre burst open. Dr Shard gasped and looked up as Mr Mulciber, with the instincts of a killer, grabbed the oscillating probe out of the doctor's hand and flung his body across Alfie's chest, preventing him from seeing who had come to his rescue.

'Stand back or the boy gets drilled!' yelled Mr Mulciber, pressing the tip of the probe against Alfie's neck and switching it on. The probe barely dragged itself through a single revolution.

'Or we could just wait until those batteries are completely dead,' said Red. 'I'm in no hurry!'

'Who are you?' barked Dr Shard.

'A friend,' said Fox. 'A friend who works best in the dark.' On his way in, Fox had grabbed a disused fire extinguisher. Producing it from behind his back and breaking the seal on the trigger, he let fly a stream of foam, which snuffed out the cooker's blue flame. 'Now I can see you, but you can't see me.'

The threat had its effect. Alfie could feel the agitation in Mr Mulciber's body as he loosened his grip on Alfie's throat and stood up. The silence was as taut as a violin string, save for the sharp exhalations of breath as Mr Mulciber and Dr Shard searched the room for their attackers.

Suddenly, like startled bats swarming from a deep cave, feet and fists came flailing out of the darkness and battered the doctor and his accomplice to the floor. Hands released Alfie's ties and he was free.

'Looks like we got here just in time,' smiled Red.

'Looks like you did,' grinned Alfie. 'I was starting to think the Luck Gene had run out.'

159

'It was Fox's idea to save you,' she said. 'I just came along for the punch up! Watch out, he's moving!'

Behind Red's back, a dazed Mr Mulciber was lifting himself up off the ground. Red swivelled and drop-kicked him back to sleep.

For the next five minutes they worked quickly as a team. Under Red's command, Fox and Alfie searched the empty building for a drip stand, two surgical masks and a tube of superglue. Unsurprisingly it was the Luckiest Boy in the World who found them.

'Still got it, then,' Fox said, winking..

'First door I opened,' said Alfie. 'There they were standing in the middle of the floor.'

While Fox and Alfie were off searching, Red used Dr Shard's bandages to tie him to Mr Mulciber. She sat both men on the floor back to back and twisted their heads until their ears were touching. When the boys returned she ran a line of superglue along the edge of the men's ears and pinched them together until they were stuck, then rigged up the drip stand, the surgical masks and the high-speed oscillating probe into a mechanical instrument of torture.

'Wake them up,' she ordered Fox. He

160

tipped the tepid ragout sauce over their heads and laughed as they spluttered back to life.

'Now then, gentlemen,' said Red. 'I have rigged up the probe in this hammock so that should the electricity come back on, the probe will start immediately. The vibrations will then cause it to slide along the pole like a knight's lance until it enters your ear, Dr Shard, and sucks out your brain. Hopefully it will still have the momentum to keep probing until it passes out through your other ear and into *your* head, Mr Mulciber.'

'Nice work,' chuckled Fox.

'Thank you,' said Red. 'Alfie, what do you think?'

Alfie wasn't quite sure what he thought. Before he'd watched her build this brain tunnelling toy he'd had Red down as a homemaker, cooking chicken, looking after Fox. Now he wasn't so certain. There was a feistier side to her. Red the fighter; Red the Revenger; Red the Magnificent!

'It's brilliant!' said Alfie admiringly.

'You won't get away with this!' snarled Mr Mulciber.

'We *will* if nobody comes to rescue you before the power comes back on,' said Red. 'Let's go!' Fox was halfway to the door when Alfie raised his hand.

161

'Before we do,' he said, 'I've got a question for Dr Shard.'

'We shouldn't be staying here, Alfie.'

'It's just a quick one. Dr Shard, you invented the Luck Gene. You know what it's capable of doing. So why did you think that the Luck Gene would let you take my brain?'

'Nobody ever listens!' shrieked the doctor. 'When good luck dances into a room, bad luck is never far behind, swishing its bushy tail of death.'

'You thought the good luck might have turned bad?'

'Alfie,' called Red. 'There's no time for this now.'

'There is always a tipping point!' shouted the doctor. 'For everyone else except me, good luck *always* leads to bad. It's just a question of time.'

Red grabbed Alfie's arm and dragged him towards the door.

'We need to get out of here,' she urged. But they were too late. As they opened the door the room lit up with torch beams and their path was blocked by the wall-like frame of Inspector Champion.

'Mr Fox and Miss Red,' he said pompously. 'Thank you for saving me the trouble of the capture.'

As he stepped into the room, however,

two big Bo Peeps in pink pushed him out of the way. Hecate and Mohana had eyes only for their Household Drudge.

Alfie snapped out of his trance and screamed in horror when he saw his aunts bearing down on him. He had just had one near-death experience—he didn't have the stomach for another. Their lips were cold and wet and made his flesh shiver as they gathered him up with stage-managed delight and hugged him to their powdered breasts.

'Alfie!' they cried. 'How we've missed you!'

'Not *me*,' Alfie muttered, as he was crushed like an ant between two rose macaroons. 'How you've missed my shopping and cleaning and beauty treatments, you mean!'

As if to prove his point, Hecate and Mohana suddenly spotted Dr Shard and Mr Mulciber tied up on the floor. They abandoned Alfie mid-hug and picked up instead two stainless steel kidney bowls from Dr Shard's trolley.

'It's those wicked men who took our photo in the bath,' hissed Hecate.

'And wouldn't stay for supper!' snarled Mohana, with a look of such contempt that it was clear to Alfie which transgression the sisters considered the worse. 'We warned

163

you what would happen if we ever found you again.'

Then they attacked Dr Shard and Mr Mulciber with all the strength that their chicken-bone arms could muster, beating them around the head and shoulders until they begged for mercy.

'Are you sure your aunts are as bad as you say they are?' Fox whispered to Alfie. 'I mean they must be reasonably fond of you, otherwise they wouldn't be dishing out quite such a thrashing.'

'They're not punishing them for nearly eating *me,*' he explained. 'They're paying them back for not wanting to marry *them.*'

Inspector Champion took advantage of the fracas to arrest Alfie.

'Everyone thinks they can cheat the long arm of the law, and nobody can,' he said, puffing out his chest like a bullfrog. 'Not when the arm in question is *mine.* In years to come, Alfie Pluck, you'll be proud of this moment. It's not every villain who can say that they've been arrested by one of the legends of the force; Sherlock Holmes, Slipper of the Yard, Inspector Champion!'

*   *   *

Twenty minutes later, the press and TV cameras were gathered in the car park outside the hospital waiting for their first sighting of the World's Luckiest Boy. Lily Quick had dashed over from the site of the shuttle crash. She was still touching up her lipstick when the cameraman counted her into shot.

'And going live in three seconds, two, one . . .'

'The manhunt is finally over,' she said, looking into the camera. 'The ruggedly good-looking Inspector Champion has captured Alfie Pluck, the boy who ate the Lucky Hen. The deranged inventor of the Luck Gene, Doctor Shard, and his ex-champion egg-guzzling henchman, Mr Mulciber, have also been taken into custody on a charge of kidnapping and attempted digestion.

'Alfie Pluck's best friends—a twenty-five-year-old, titian-haired chicken-fryer called Red and her younger brother Fox, a boy who last brushed his hair, apparently, when dinosaurs roamed the Earth—will be charged with the lesser crime of obstructing the police. We understand that Alfie Pluck's only living relatives, Hecate and Mohana Pluck, will continue to look after Alfie once he has been assessed by police doctors. This is Lily Quick telling it like it is, outside St Flukes Hospital.'

As she finished, Inspector Champion

made what he thought was a triumphant entrance, leading his captives out of the hospital to a grateful world. He waved his hands above his head like a Roman Emperor, and was only slightly peeved that nobody had thought to play 'We are the Champions' by Queen as a fitting musical tribute to him. It was also mildly galling that the cameras were only interested in Alfie.

Suddenly a limousine with blacked out windows screeched into the car park and slewed to a halt in front of Alfie. It trapped Alfie, Red and Fox on one side of the car and the Inspector, the aunts and Dr Shard and Mr Mulciber on the other. The rear door flew open and a chinless man in a smart suit stepped out. He was wringing his hands and clearly nervous.

'Alfie Pluck?' said the Minister for Selling Bad News As If It Was Brilliant. 'Get in. The Prime Minister wants to see you.'

'Who are you?' challenged Red.

'Back off!' said the Minister. 'You're not involved.'

He grabbed Alfie's shoulder and pushed him inside the car. Then he shouted 'Drive!' at the top of his voice and the limousine sped off. The whole kidnap, for that was what it appeared to be, had taken less than ten seconds.

Hecate and Mohana were stunned into silence as their slave was snatched from under their noses; Inspector Champion was insulted that all his efforts to capture Alfie would now go unrewarded; and Fox and Red . . .

'They've gone!'

Inspector Champion's cry of despair echoed around the car park. His victory parade, which had started with an impressive tally of five prisoners, was already down to two—one of whom was a mummified madman, and another who stank of bad eggs. Maybe today would not be the day Inspector Champion got promotion after all.

CHAPTER SEVENTEEN

Shuttle *Relentless* had ploughed a furrow through six miles of light industrial warehousing before belly-flopping into the middle of the O2 Arena. Arc lights illuminated the smoking wreckage and efficient-looking people in white radiation suits walked in and out of the main shuttle door carrying clipboards and containers billowing with icy smoke.

On a pile of debris a short distance away from the doorway to the craft, sat a small figure, shoulders hunched forward, head in hands.

'That's her,' said the Minister for Selling Bad News As If It Was Brilliant. 'Just go up and introduce yourself. She's expecting you.'

Alfie was reluctant.

'She won't bite,' the Minister joked. 'She can't! She's just had all her teeth removed by the latest opinion poll result.'

Alfie wondered what sort of opinion poll extracted every tooth in a person's head. An opinion poll of angry dentists perhaps.

Marjorie Lentless was muttering to herself as he approached.

'This is the end of me. Lowest ever rating for a serving Prime Minister in eighty years, hated by old and young alike, and now this.' She raised her head and howled at the chunk of steaming metal in front of her. 'They told me you would fly!'

Alfie coughed to let her know that she was not alone.

'Oh,' she said, standing up and patting her hair into shape. 'Alfie Pluck. Good of you to come and give an old failure some advice.'

She held out her hand, but Alfie refused to take it. The Minister for Selling Bad News As If It Was Brilliant had lied.

Marjorie Lentless had a mouthful of teeth.

'Are you going to eat my brain?' he asked bluntly, deciding he'd better get it over with.

'I'm not hungry,' she said.

Alfie didn't laugh.

'Politician's joke. Not very funny. Sorry.' She sat back down on the lump of twisted metal and tapped the seat beside her. 'The thing is,' she confessed, 'I *thought* I could eat your brain, but I can't.'

'It's not allowed, is it,' he said, 'eating other people?'

'It's not that,' she said, 'I just don't think it's a vote winner. Now that you're famous and people know who you are and what you can do, somebody would notice if you went missing. It's what we in politics call a no-brainer.' Her second attempt at a joke went the same way as the first.

'Nonetheless,' Alfie said. 'I think I should warn you that if you change your mind your chances of actually getting my brain out of my skull are slim. A couple of people have tried and the Luck Gene saw them off.' He deliberately didn't mention the warning from Dr Shard that at some point his good luck would turn bad just in case she spotted a chink in his armour.

'Thank you for telling me,' she said.

'So why am I here?' asked Alfie.

169

'Because there's something I'd like you to do for me,' she said. 'Have you ever heard of the feelgood factor?'

The Prime Minister went on to explain that the people of Britain needed a boost to make them feel better about themselves and when they felt better about themselves, they'd feel better about her and vote her back in.

'So what do you have in mind?' he asked.

'Well, you're British,' she said casually, 'and you're the Luckiest Boy in the World. Winning Wimbledon has been mentioned.'

'I don't play tennis,' he replied.

'What about golf?'

Alfie shook his head. 'The only sport I've ever played was snail racing in my dog's kennel. That's not going to do it, is it?'

She banged her fist on the metal seat.

'There must be something you can do to lift the country's spirits!'

Alfie wanted to give her an answer, he really did. She had an extraordinary knack of making *her* failure seem like *his*.

'Well this may sound silly,' he said, steeling himself to be bold. 'But maybe it's not what *I* can do, but what *you* can do instead. If you're as unpopular as you say you are, wouldn't it raise the country's spirits if you just resigned?'

Her jaw dropped.

'How does resigning get me re-elected?' he barked.

'Oh yes. I hadn't thought of that,' said Alfie, who wasn't one hundred per cent sure how an election worked.

'Any more suggestions like that,' she added tersely, 'and I *will* eat your brains for breakfast.' This time Alfie laughed.

'That one wasn't a joke,' she said with a face as grim as a headmistress seeing her pants up a flagpole.

Just then a scream came from inside the shuttle. Alfie looked round as three scientists rushed out through the airlock. One tripped and fell to the ground, but the others ran on. When Alfie bent to offer his arm to the one who had tripped she looked straight up at him with terrified eyes, then scrambled to her feet and fled the way of her colleagues, leaving Alfie and the Prime Minister alone.

The dark interior of the space craft suddenly lit up. Alfie's eyes took a moment to adjust, but when they did, he saw that the halo of light was spotted with wraith-like figures walking towards him. The creatures had translucent, balloon-shaped bodies, like squid. They shrank and elongated all the time. Up and down, up and down like lungs breathing. Tentacles swirled either side of the body, and

171

underneath a flap of skin that hung round their midriff like a short skirt they had three legs, a tripodal structure that span continuously like a propeller and kept them floating above the ground.

It wasn't until one of them spoke that Alfie realised it had a face. The creature's features lived inside its stomach. Peeping out through the semi-transparent skin it looked like a person trapped in ice. It had huge almond-shaped eyes, a circular mouth, ear-holes like tiny whirlpools and saggy cheeks which flapped down on either side of its mouth like badly hung curtains. Despite its otherworld-ugliness Alfie was entranced by its benign grace.

'Hello,' said the creature. 'Forgive me if I titillate the wrong words, but I am using a localised vocalised translator which can often be too literal for its own god.'

Alfie had no words in reply, just wide-eyed awe and disbelief.

Luckily there was a politician on hand, because the one thing a politician *does* have in abundance is words. Marjorie Lentless ran towards Alfie and hugged him like a little girl who'd just been given a pony.

'Oh, Alfie!' she cried, her face wreathed in a smile. 'You're a genius.'

'And who are you, Ancient?' asked the

alien.

'Not so much of the ancient!' she said, bristling. 'Marjorie Lentless, Prime Minister of Great Britain.' She extended her hand to shake the creature's tentacle. 'This is Alfie Pluck, and you are?'

'Commander Mmnnaarg,' said the creature. 'I am a Quirk from the planet Fortuna in the galaxy of Boon-Boon. We've been here previous,' it said, 'when Good Queen Beth was reigning, which is when we lost one of our pretties. We was combing back to tackle him home when we broke down.'

'Three hundred years later!' exclaimed the Prime Minister.

'Time is a human construct,' said Commander Mmnnaarg. 'Three hundred years to us is but a tadpole's toot in a puddle.'

Alfie couldn't stop himself from laughing.

'Did you mean to say that?' he asked. 'Or was that the localised vocalised translator muddling your words again?'

'No, I meant to say that,' said the gentle alien. 'We have very windy tadpoles on Fortuna and extremely large puddles. But enough, you must want to know why we are here. Our speck chip broke down on the dark side of the moon and we was up shark creek without a paddle until *your* speck shovel flew past and we were able to hitch a lift. We are a lucky breed, and as a result, here we is now.'

'I can see all of you,' said Marjorie Lentless looking around, 'but where is your space ship?'

'In our minds,' said the creature, gesturing towards its fellow aliens. 'We are unique in having a Garage Cortex in our brains. If we use our combination knowledge to fixillate the broken craft *together,* the fixillating gets done in no time at all.'

'Well, whatever it is you're saying I think you're magnificent!' cried the Prime Minister with undisguised delight. 'In fact, I have never seen a more wonderful sight in my life!' She felt drunk with happiness. 'Would you mind awfully waiting right there, while I have a private word with Alfie?'

'Be my ghost,' said the Quirk, bowing graciously.

The Prime Minister knelt in front of Alfie, clasped his face between her hands and kissed him on the nose.

'I can't thank you enough!' she said. 'This is just the piece of luck I needed. Name me one other country on the planet that's got aliens from outer space as a tourist attraction? This has justified snatching all that money away from hospitals and schools, and shooting it up into space. This has *made* me!'

Alfie thought there was something slightly unhinged about the way she clasped his shoulders so tightly and shook him like a rag doll. 'Thanks to ME, Britain will be the focus of the world, and I shall be remembered for ever and ever!'

'And what about me?' asked Alfie. 'What's to happen to me?'

'You're to go home, of course.'

'Home?' That was an unwelcome word. Marjorie Lentless noticed the hesitancy in Alfie's voice.

'As a hero,' she said, sweetening the pill, 'safe in the knowledge that nobody from my government will ever chase you again.'

'And what if I don't want to go home?' he asked. 'I've still got to find Bandit.'

'Who's Bandit?'

'My best friend. He was kidnapped by a three-legged greyhound called Tallulah.' The Prime Minister frowned.

'He's a dog.'

'Oh, is that all?' she said. 'We'll buy you another one.'

'I don't want another one. And I don't want to live with my aunts again. You can't make me.'

'You're behaving like a child,' she said

briskly.

'That's because I am one,' he said. 'They treat me like a slave.'

'Well, do you have anywhere else to go?'

That was the sixty-four million dollar question.

Unfortunately, Alfie only had a six-cent answer.

'There's a den on the common,' he said hopefully.

'A den!' she exclaimed. 'Made out of what?'

'Wood and stuff,' said Alfie. 'Leaves, moss . . . there's a tarpaulin on the ground to stop the damp rising.'

'I'm the Prime Minister of a First World country,' she cried. 'I can't have children running about our parks and commons living in dens. This isn't the Stone Age. My name is Marjorie Lentless not Ug! No.'

'What do you mean, no?' he said. 'I just found you some aliens! You can't just say no to the Luckiest Boy in the World.'

'You're still a boy,' she reminded him, 'and as such you will do as you're told.'

Alfie recognised an order when he heard one. He was going home. The Prime Minister must have seen his shoulders slump, however, because she softened the corners of her mouth and tried to be kind.

'What I mean is that if you're as lucky as

176

you say you are, something will turn up. For the time being though, you have to go home.' Alfie had no answer for this. He noticed that the Luck Gene didn't either. He was waiting for a great big dollop of luck to fall from the sky and put a stop to his return to Mire Road. But dollops came there none.

The Prime Minister's parting promise of a knighthood did nothing to lighten Alfie's mood in the limousine on the way back to Mire Road. Maybe this was what Dr Shard meant about the tipping point. Had his good luck just tipped over into bad? If it had, he'd *never* escape from his aunts.

He was sharing the back seat of the car with the Minister for Selling Bad News As If It Was Brilliant, who had recently been promoted to Minister for Brilliant Alien Landings Which Reflect Only Glory On Our Great Leader.

'Are you powerful?' Alfie asked him.

'Some might say,' said the man, whose scrawny neck somehow reminded Alfie of the Lucky Hen.

'I thought you must be,' said Alfie. 'Or you wouldn't have a car like this.'

The Minister laughed. 'Appearances can be deceptive. Sometimes I don't feel very powerful at all.'

'When?' asked Alfie.

'When the Prime Minister shouts at me,' he whispered.

'It's the same with my aunts,' said Alfie. 'Everyone thinks they're really nice to me, but that's just a front. They only want me back because they hate doing stuff for themselves. In that house I'm not a person, I'm just their Household Drudge.' He turned to face the Minister for Brilliant Alien Landings Which Reflect Only Glory On Our Great Leader and spoke in a deliberately slow voice. 'I don't want to go back and live with them.'

The Minister shifted uneasily in his seat.

'You can't always have what you want, Alfie.'

'But that's mad! I'm the Luckiest Boy in the World. I should be able to do whatever I want whenever I want to do it . . . and I can't even choose where I live. Couldn't you pass a law that says I am forbidden to live with my aunts?' He suddenly had an idea. 'You could stop the car and let me run away.'

'No I couldn't,' said the Minister. 'I'd lose my job if I lost you.'

Alfie sat back and sighed.

'I don't think I want to be lucky any more,' he said, 'all it seems to do is make me miserable.'

'We're all miserable,' said the Minister,

speaking from his heart. 'Life's about getting on with it, Alfie. Making your own luck; making the best of a bad job.'

'So you won't help?' said Alfie. This powerful man was as useless as everyone else—like a wet tissue at a funeral.

True to form, he avoided answering the question. 'Do as you're told,' he said. 'Toe the line. And things won't be so bad, you'll see.'

As a tugboat bellowed like a melancholic whale, the limousine plunged into the Blackwall Tunnel and disappeared from view.

Alfie felt as though he was going back in time to a life he thought he'd left behind. Being the Luckiest Boy in the World meant nothing. He was no better off now than he had been before he ate that chicken. Doctor Shard was right—when good luck danced into a room, bad luck was never far behind, swishing its bushy tail of death.

CHAPTER EIGHTEEN

From the moment he arrived home Alfie's good luck seemed to vanish. His one hope had been that being the Luckiest Boy in the World, luckless people would bash down his door begging him to solve their problems. He reasoned that if he was busy being helpful he wouldn't have time to be a Household Drudge. But Alfie's star had been eclipsed by the aliens in more ways than one. Incredibly, during the Quirks' first health check, scientists made an astonishing discovery:

THE DAILY SNEER
Friday April 21st

QUIRK BRAIN HARDWIRED FOR LUCK
[By Science Correspondent—Tessa Tube]

Can you believe it? Baby Quirks are born with the Luck Gene already installed . . .

When he read this headline, Alfie's worst fears were realised. He was no longer unique. While the lucky aliens became the most talked-about creatures in the country, occupying thousands of front pages of newspapers and hundreds of television and radio interviews, Alfie was forgotten. He was just an ordinary-looking lucky boy; the aliens were freakish-looking lucky monsters from a different universe. No contest. The public liked their celebrities freakish and different, and as the Prime Minister needed the public's vote she shamelessly used the aliens to promote her campaign. When they weren't opening supermarkets, judging bonny baby contests, or attending film premieres, the aliens were appearing at election rallies with Marjorie Lentless. With the Quirks at her side, millions poured out onto the streets to meet her and her popularity soared.

*   *   *

Hecate and Mohana were delighted to have Alfie back to being their full-time Household Drudge. Motivated by mean-spirited revenge, they spent each day devising new ways to exhaust him so that never again would he have the strength to run away and leave them lying in the bath. They found millions of pointless time-wasting jobs for him to do; washing nailbrushes, polishing walnuts, folding stamps, chasing silverfish, dusting shadows and sitting in the bath as a bath plug. They used his knees, back and shoulders as a step ladder, his fingers as coat pegs, his tongue as a flycatcher, his hair as a mop, his voice as an answer-phone, his skin as a note pad and his lungs as a portable vacuum cleaner. And at night, when he was too tired to walk, they wrecked his sleep by stuffing pots and pans into his straw mattress, making it so lumpy that he was forced to lie on the cold concrete floor.

Alfie grew more and more miserable. He resigned himself to the fact that the Luck Gene had simply stopped working. Unable to leave the house, he found himself thinking about Fox and Red and wondering where they were. In prison, probably, unless Fox had already masterminded their escape. Would he ever see them again? Would he ever see Bandit again either? He hoped so, but had his doubts. In those restless early-morning hours when he was alone in the cellar with nothing but his thoughts for company, he would close his eyes and talk to his Luck Gene.

'If you're still there, Luck Gene, there are two things I really want you to do. One; bring back Bandit and two; make Fox and Red be outside with a sledgehammer so they can break down the door and hide me in the walk-in chicken fridge at Chango's Chicken Shack.'

Night after night he waited for luck to ride to his rescue, but it never came.

CHAPTER NINETEEN

One Monday morning, ten weeks after the space shuttle crash-landed on top of the O2 Arena and two weeks before the General Election, Alfie's luck changed. He was ironing Hecate's and Mohana's newspapers, when the lead story caught his eye.

THE DAILY SNEER
Monday July 3rd

ONE OF OUR QUIRKS IS ILL!
[By Entertainment Correspondent — Lily Quick]

Yesterday morning, the alien visitor known as Nellftardi was struck down by a mystery illness when he fell asleep twenty-three times in six minutes on the *Breakfast Time* sofa.

At 08.42 Nellftardi was rushed to hospital, where doctors were baffled by the alien's symptoms.

After extensive tests a hospital spokesman announced that the doctors were pretty sure it was either Swine Flu or Chicken Flu or Pig Flu or Cow Flu or Bat Flu or Cat Flu or Dog Flu or Alien Flu. And if it wasn't one of those, it was something similar. They didn't know.

By 10 o'clock the Prime Minister was forced to deny that she had been the cause of the alien's illness.

'The idea that I have exploited the aliens and their good nature to gain publicity for myself in the run up to the election is a slanderous accusation. They *wanted* to be involved and get first-hand experience of democracy in action. They didn't have to criss-cross the country on my Battle Bus. They chose to. And in fact they developed quite a taste for stale biscuits and stewed tea.'

For the next hour the alien's illness remained a mystery until the Quirks sent a

spokesalien out onto the hospital steps to explain what was wrong.

'We love it here in Great Brigand,' Commander Mmnnaarg said through his localised vocalised translator, 'but we have been away from our planet for a long time, and the truth is that Nellftardi is homevomit. In fact all of us are homevomit and if we don't go home soon we will all end up in horse-spittle.'

Just as soon as they had found their lost crewman from the sixteenth century and their speck chip was fixillated in the Garage Cortex of their minds, the Quirks were going home.

Unbeknownst to Alfie, the Prime Minister and her ministers had been in emergency session all night debating the implications of this terrifying development. Without the aliens to bring her luck, Marjorie Lentless feared that she would lose the election.

'Popularity always comes down to charisma,' said the Minister for Honesty. 'Without the aliens to attract the crowds, you clearly haven't got it. What you need is another lucky mascot.'

*   *   *

The doorbell rang just as Alfie was finishing the article. He was not allowed to open the door without his aunts present in case he tried to run away, so he waited in the hall until Hecate and Mohana tumbled downstairs wearing matching pink pyjamas and statically-charged dressing gowns with pom-poms on the sleeves.

Mohana drew back the bolts.

'Who is it?' she shouted through the door.

'The Prime Minister,' a voice replied.

Hecate and Mohana hissed like two snakes.

'I knew this would happen,' whispered Hecate. 'That witch of a Prime Minister wants to take Alfie away from us. What shall we do?'

'We could pretend we're not here.'

'But she's already heard your voice.'

'We could say we've got the plague!'

The doorbell rang again.

'It is rather urgent!' shouted a man outside. 'We've got an important election to win in less than two weeks' time.'

Mohana stood on Alfie's toes.

'Don't move!' she said, as she turned the latch and opened the door.

The Prime Minister strode into the hall without waiting to be asked. She was followed by the Minister for Honesty, and the ever-attentive Minister for Brilliant Alien Landings Which Reflect Only Glory On Our Great Leader. Looking extremely tired and irritable, Marjorie Lentless pointed her finger at Alfie and said, 'Alfie Pluck. Your country needs you.'

'No, it doesn't,' cried Hecate. 'We need him more.'

'Can we speak in private?' The Prime Minister made a move towards the lounge, but the aunts stopped her in her tracks.

'No!' Mohana bellowed. 'Alfie stays where we can see him.'

'Very well,' said the Minister for Brilliant Alien Landings Which Reflect Only Glory On Our Great Leader. 'It won't have escaped your notice that since the Quirks hitched their wagon to the Prime Minister's Battle Bus she has enjoyed a rise in popularity. Now that they are going home, she needs to replace them.'

'That's ridiculous,' sneered Hecate. 'Where are you going to find more aliens?'

'They mean me,' said Alfie. He felt his heart leap as he said it. Was the aliens' misfortune his lucky break? It wasn't

187

possible to be in two places at once. If he was out helping the Prime Minister win the election he couldn't be at home being a slave. 'I'll do it,' he said.

'No, you won't,' barked Mohana. 'We are your aunts and we forbid it.'

'And I'm the Prime Minister,' said Marjorie Lentless, smiling. 'I win!'

Alfie was ecstatic. He had been pulled back from the jaws of eternal drudgery. But it was not all good news, because the Prime Minister had a little task for him.

'Tomorrow morning I shall announce that this Wednesday is to be a surprise holiday for the whole nation.'

'There is nothing the great British public likes more than a day off work,' interjected the Minister for Honesty.

'Quite so,' said the Prime Minister. 'It is my belief that a day of general laziness will guarantee me victory in the election. I had intended to take the Quirks back to the spot where all of this began, to the Dorchester Hotel in Park Lane, where they would perform several death-defying stunts to amaze the crowds with their luck.'

'You mean like standing the aliens under a falling tree and watching the branches miss them by a whisker?' asked Alfie. 'Or tying a heavy anvil round their necks, throwing them off London Bridge and

188

watching them plummet safely onto the deck of a passing coal barge?'

'Exactly that,' said the Minister for Brilliant Alien Landings Which Reflect Only Glory On Our Great Leader. 'And firing them from a cannonball into a tank full of hungry piranhas and watching the start of a second Ice Age freeze the water before they go in.'

That *would* be lucky, thought Alfie.

'Now that they are going home,' said the Prime Minister, 'we think it would be more appropriate if we simply used the event to say farewell to our alien friends and wish them luck for the future. They are obviously tired and emotional, and it would not be to our benefit if one of them lost concentration and died horribly on live television.'

'Go on,' said Alfie, unsure where all this was leading.

'So we thought that you could do it instead.'

'Do what?'

'Defy death,' she smiled. 'Alfie dear, I'd like you to provide the climax to the proceedings, the highlight of the day that will make you a celebrity once again and fix the memory of my generosity into every voter's mind.'

'How?' he asked nervously.

189

'By recreating the Lucky Hen's famous walk through the Park Lane traffic.'

'No no no no!' shrieked Hecate. 'No! What if he doesn't come back?' Alfie was thinking exactly the same thing. 'What if he's squashed like a bug on a windscreen?'

'But he won't be,' said Marjorie Lentless.

'I might,' gulped Alfie.

'He's right,' said the Minister for Honesty. 'He's only a slip of a lad. It wouldn't take much to splat him.'

The Prime Minister held up her hand. 'He is the Luckiest Boy in the World,' she said. 'It won't happen. Besides, this day may be about you, the aliens and the Luck Gene, but it's also about me, Alfie. Do you honestly think I would put my career on the line if I didn't think it was completely safe?' The Minister for Honesty was about to say 'yes' when the Prime Minister stayed his tongue with a dagger of a look.

*   *   *

So it was that Marjorie Lentless's Holiday of Luck was conceived. A car would pick up Alfie and his aunts on Wednesday morning and take them to the Dorchester Hotel where Alfie would 'Walk Park Lane' at 12 o'clock in front of an estimated television audience of sixty million viewers.

Alfie's brain was a jumble of conflicting emotions as he tried to make sense of the Prime Minister's whirlwind visit.

Hecate and Mohana, on the other hand, knew exactly what they were feeling: fury . . . at the prospect of losing their Household Drudge again. If Alfie succeeded in dodging the cars in front of an audience that large he would become an international superstar, and once he'd tasted lobster on the French Riviera he'd be far too grand to come home and make beans on toast for them.

'Please don't go!' simpered Hecate, fluttering her eyes like a fawning dog.

But Alfie wanted to go. He wanted to be famous, because famous people didn't have to live with their wicked aunts. Famous people stayed in posh hotels with comfy beds. He didn't say this though.

'You know I really want to stay here painting your feet with creosote to stop your rampant foot-fungus from spreading any further,' he said, 'but sadly I don't have a choice. It's what the Prime Minister wants.'

'Well what the Prime Minister wants,' snarled Mohana, 'the Prime Minister does not always get.' The two sisters pushed Alfie into the cellar, locked the door, then went upstairs and plotted till dawn.

Alfie didn't sleep. He was trying to work out the odds for his survival. Ten weeks ago when he had escaped a full lobotomy at the hands of Dr Shard thanks to a lucky space-craft crash, he'd have said his chances were one hundred per cent. But now, after weeks of drudgery and no sign of relief he wasn't so confident. Admittedly the Prime Minister had thrown him a lifeline by inviting him to participate in her Holiday of Luck, but was the line attached to a boat or would he simply float off towards the horizon? What odds now? Twenty-five per cent? Ten? Zero, even? He could step off that pavement and be killed by the first passing car.

So was it worth the risk? Yes. Of that Alfie had never been more certain. If the Luck Gene *was* still working, he would never have to pander to his aunts' cruel whims again.

*   *   *

Early next morning, Hecate and Mohana refused to unlock Alfie from the cellar to prevent him from ear-wigging their very private phone conversation.

'Hello. Is that Inspector Champion?'

'Yes,' said the voice at the other end of the line. 'Who's this?'

'Only your favourite helicopter co-pilots,' said Mohana in a husky voice she hoped sounded alluring.

'Oh . . .' came the thoroughly dejected reply. 'What can I do for you?'

'Do you remember in the helicopter, Inspector, when you said something about wanting a slice of the Luck Gene?'

'Vaguely,' he said.

'We were wondering if you could lay your hands on Dr Shard and Mr Mulciber?'

An hour later, Alfie heard a car pull up outside the house. There was a gentle knock on the front door, five sets of feet crossed the hall into the sitting room and the door closed. Alfie knew something was going on, but even if he'd guessed for a thousand years he would never have imagined anything half as despicable as the truth.

*   *   *

The aunts sat their visitors in a businesslike circle, then thanked Inspector Champion for coming.

'It's nice to see that everyone has their price,' Mohana said with a coquettish smile.

'I've done nothing illegal yet,' he said

defensively. 'Just taken two prisoners out of their cells for a couple of hours of compassionate leave.' He looked at his watch. 'We've got less than ninety minutes. I suggest we crack on.'

Mohana took charge and explained their little problem. 'Marjorie Lentless's Holiday of Luck is going to make Alfie bigger than Elvis. After it's beamed around the world, everyone will want to meet him.'

'Your point is?' asked Dr Shard, whose bones had healed sufficiently for his bandages to have been removed. The stress of losing a fortune had taken its toll on his face, however. His mouth was twisted into a permanent sneer; grey bags flapped under his eyes; and his wild hair was bone white. He had turned into a sour old man with nothing left to lose.

'Our point is that we need him here as our Household Drudge!' shrieked Hecate. 'That's what we got him for in the first place. It's not fair!'

Mohana gently brushed her sister's wrist to calm her down.

'We have been doing some thinking,' she said serenely, 'and we have identified the problem as the Luck Gene. For as long as it remains inside his head, the Prime Minister will want him for her holiday stunt and global superstardom will inevitably follow.'

'And we will lose our slave forever,' squealed Hecate.

'Most regrettable,' said Dr Shard.

'So we've come up with a plan,' Mohana said, scrunching her shoulders with childish glee. 'We were wondering if you'd be interested in us Serving Alfie up to you on a plate, so to speak?'

'You mean cook him?' asked Mr Mulciber.

Inspector Champion, who had been on edge since he arrived, jumped up from his chair.

'I'm sorry,' he blurted out. 'I know I'm here of my own accord, but how can you do this to your own flesh and blood?'

'Who said he's our flesh and blood?' said Mohana, smiling eerily.

'We found him at a bus stop,' giggled Hecate. 'Wrapped up in a basket. Abandoned by his mother. And we'd always talked about having a slave-child to look after us in our old age. So we took him.'

While Inspector Champion froze with disbelief, Mohana attacked.

'Close your mouth, you big baby.' The Inspector was struggling with his conscience. Should he stay or should he go? If he left he might never get lucky again. He stayed and sat down.

'Our plan does NOT involve the eating of the whole brain, nor the killing of Alfie,' she continued. 'We propose to give you access to the boy and in exchange you will only take the bit of his brain with the Luck Gene in.'

'To stop other people wanting him,' clarified Hecate. 'Leaving the rest of his brain—the bit that loves Household Drudgery—to us.'

'I'm in!' said Mr Mulciber, with vulgar haste.

'Not so fast,' said Dr Shard. 'We can't help anybody while we're still in police custody.' Mohana turned to the policeman and curled her lips like a cunning crocodile.

'This is where you come in, Inspector.'

'You want me to release the prisoners and drop all charges?'

'Only *you* can do it, Inspector.'

'Not for much longer,' he said bitterly. This comment took everyone by surprise. 'I lost three prisoners from that hospital car park. Even though one of them *did* turn out to be a National Treasure, it's brought my career to a rather premature end. I've been retired. With no pension. From the end of this week.'

'Then all the more reason to get on with

it,' said Hecate. 'The Holiday of Luck is tomorrow. We must do this tonight.'

Inspector Champion stood up and attempted to reestablish his authority.

'I *could* drop the charges against Mr Mulciber and Dr Shard and release them,' he said, 'but I need to know what's in it for me.'

Mohana and Hecate exchanged a well-rehearsed glance.

'We were thinking, Inspector, that maybe you could have a third of the Luck Gene . . .' With their thickly painted lips the aunts pouted alluringly at Dr Shard and Mr Mulciber, '. . . if the other two gentlemen are amenable.'

Dr Shard leant across the coffee table.

'As creator of the Luck Gene it is I alone who will be eating it, Inspector, but the wealth I shall acquire from being lucky belongs to me and Mr Mulciber. For releasing us with no charge, I see no reason why we should not stretch to a third share of this fortune.' He held out his hand. 'Are we all agreed?'

After the treacherous plot had been sealed, Mr Mulciber was keen to get on with the extraction.

'The boy is in the cellar. Let's do it now,' he said, drooling excitedly.

But Inspector Champion called a halt.

197

The prisoners were due back at the police station in twenty minutes and good behaviour was crucial to securing their early release. Eating Alfie's brain would take place that night.

'Hang a sign on the door of Alfie's bedroom so that we know where he's sleeping,' said Mr Mulciber as they departed into the rain with a duplicate set of house keys. 'Leave the rest to us!'

*   *   *

Alfie heard nothing of this conversation. He did hear the guests leave, however, and the cellar door being unlocked.

'Good morning, Alfie,' Hecate called down the steps in a saccharine-sweet voice she usually saved for wild birds in the garden. 'How would you like to move upstairs into your own bedroom, with a real bed and a nameplate on the door?'

Alfie was too tired to resist. He followed his aunts up the stairs, waited on the landing while Hecate moved her things into Mohana's bedroom and hung a cardboard sign on her old bedroom door that said: ALFIE'S ROOM. Then he fell into Hecate's soft pillow and slept for the rest of the day.

CHAPTER TWENTY

When Alfie woke up at 6 o'clock that evening he was still tired. Just as well, because three hours later his aunts insisted he go back to bed again. Even stranger, they were being *nice* to him. Alfie was suspicious. They seemed to have forgotten about the bedtime tasks that they normally expected him to perform, such as flossing their false teeth, lubricating Mohana's eyeball and vacuuming their beds for bed bugs. They were flitting around the house like two demented bluebottles doing all of the jobs that for years they had sworn they didn't know how to do; filling him a bath, cooking him eggy toast and making him cocoa.

'What's going on?' he asked. 'Why am I the one sitting down at the kitchen table being waited on?'

'Nothing,' said Hecate. 'It's a big day tomorrow, that's all. Marjorie Lentless's Holiday of Luck . . . we're so excited!'

'We want you to do the best you can,' added Mohana, taking the lid off a tarnished silver salver and presenting another tasty tit-bit. 'Lobster sandwich?'

Clearly something was afoot. Alfie had

not spent all that time in Fox's company without realising that human beings were devious creatures who smiled to your face as they stabbed you in the back. That sign on his door was fishy too. Tonight, sleep was a luxury he couldn't afford. He would have to stay alert. Unfortunately the hot cocoa was already taking its effect, and after his aunts had tucked him up in bed and switched off the light, he was soon asleep, surrendering himself to a dream about hedgehogs playing chicken on a busy dual carriageway.

* * *

As luck would have it, the front door creaked and the noise woke Alfie up. He sprang forward in his bed and listened in the darkness. It was the middle of the night and there was somebody in the house. Hearing whispered voices in the hall, Alfie swung his legs out of bed, quietly made his way to the door, and poked his head outside onto the landing. The lights were off in Mohana's room, but he could hear his aunts giggling. Downstairs, the voices sounded horribly familiar. Something was not right. The sign on his bedroom door was troubling him too. *He* knew where he was sleeping, *his aunts* knew where he was sleeping, who else needed to know? He unhooked the string from the drawing pin, tip-toed to the banisters and peered into the hall. Even from above he recognised the bald head of Dr Shard and the greasy locks of Mr Mulciber, but seeing the heroic shoulders of Inspector Champion came as a surprise. Sitting in the hall on a wheeled trolley was the high-speed oscillating ear probe and next to it, wrapped up in newspaper, Alfie could make out the frying pan for Mr Mulciber's brain ragout.

Now Alfie knew exactly why Mohana and Hecate had moved him up from the cellar and insisted on the sign. It wasn't a present, it was X marks the spot. It was a sign for the three brain-chefs downstairs that this was the room where they'd find their lucky meat. A despicable deal had been struck in secret and Alfie was the prize. He had to get out of the house now, that much was obvious, but he also had to buy himself time and delay his pursuers. He looked at the nameplate in his hand— ALFIE'S ROOM and hung it on the handle to Mohana's bedroom door. Then he returned to Hecate's bedroom, locked the door and tugged open the window. A cold blast of air made him shiver. He pulled a jumper over his pyjamas and stepped into his shoes, then hunted through the debris under Hecate's bed to find a black plastic bin liner, into which he shoved a few more clothes. Then Alfie threw the bag out of the window, shinned down the drainpipe and sprinted to the bottom of the garden where the shadows would hide him.

He climbed the wall into the alleyway, but still had no idea where he was headed. Perched on top, he heard his aunts scream. Seconds later he heard the three men scream as well. As much with relief as mirth, Alfie laughed. If there was one thing Hecate and Mohana loathed it was being seen in bed without their beauty aids— make up, eyes, teeth and wigs—and clearly the men agreed.

In answer to their screams, another scream echoed through the night and turned Alfie's flesh to goosebumps. The second scream had come from the common. He could just imagine the horror now. The screaming child being torn limb from limb by ripping claws and slavering teeth, those cold ruthless eyes of the werefoxes casting an innocent soul into an everlasting inferno of torment and damnation.

That was where he would go. Fox's den.

It was insane, of course, but that was why it would work. The den was empty most of the time and only Fox, Red and his tribe knew of its existence. Even if his aunts *did* know where it was they had scared him too efficiently for too many years with their gory werefox tales to expect him to take refuge *inside* the beast's lair.

It was time to throw off the shackles of fear and confront his childhood terror. He had no choice. Where else could he go? Besides, he was lucky and luck cancelled out evil every time . . . Alfie pulled himself up short. That was assuming he was still lucky. He'd find out tomorrow, wouldn't he? When it would be too late to do anything about it if he wasn't.

*   *   *

In Mohana's bedroom, Mohana and Hecate were huddled at the top of the bed clutching the duvet around their necks. In her haste, Mohana had popped her false eye in back to front. She looked like she had one eye and one white ping pong ball.

'What is it with you vile men?' she cried in anger. 'Two beautiful ladies should be free to bathe or sleep without ugly men bursting in on them willy-nilly!'

'I can assure you it was not out of choice,' said a red-faced Inspector Champion.

'It was a terrible accident,' gulped Dr Shard. 'The sign on the door led us to believe that Alfie was in here.'

'Well he isn't,' snapped Hecate.

After the three men had turned their backs and Hecate and Mohana had rearranged their faces, they decided that Alfie must have got wind of the plan and escaped. Pursuing him into the night would be a fruitless exercise and, because they knew exactly where he was going to be in the morning, they stayed where they were and came up with a new plan.

*   *   *

Fortunately Inspector Champion had been put in charge of Park Lane security again. It was to be his swansong before his retirement. This meant that he had the authority to allow Mr Mulciber's yellow cab to park inside the security ring at Marble Arch, and for an additional ambulance to park just a few hundred yards away from the entrance to the Dorchester Hotel. At this precise spot Alfie would be dicing with death by stepping off the pavement and following in the footsteps of the Lucky Hen. It was Hecate and Mohana's job to make sure that Alfie did not chicken out, so to speak.

'But what if he doesn't come home?' worried Hecate. 'How can we be sure he'll be there?'

'The whole world is waiting to see him dodge the traffic. Where's he going to hide?' said Dr Shard. 'He'll be there, because he can't be anywhere else.'

'And if he comes back?'

'Act like nothing has happened,' ordered the doctor. 'We mustn't raise his suspicions a second time.' He turned to Mr Mulciber for confirmation that he knew what he was doing. 'When the boy is halfway across Park Lane the cab will hit him,' Mr Mulciber said.

'I will immediately call forward the closest ambulance to the scene and insist that Alfie is put inside,' said Inspector Champion.

'An ambulance,' said Dr Shard, 'that I shall be driving, heavily disguised of course. I will take the boy around the corner, park up in a garage in Mayfair and proceed with the brain operation.'

'Removing only the Luck Gene,' Mohana reminded her fellow conspirators, 'and leaving behind the bits that make him good at cleaning, shopping, beautifying and generally being a First-Class Slave!'

'It's foolproof,' shrieked Hecate, forgetting the fundamental rule of all demonic plans: *Never count your chickens before they're hatched.*

*   *   *

Alfie found Fox's den eventually. It had taken some backtracking in the dark, and on two occasions he had been forced to wait for the full moon to appear from behind the clouds before he could see where he was, but at least he now had somewhere dry to lie down and think. Inside the crude shelter Alfie found two sleeping bags lying side by side, a groundsheet littered with cardboard boxes from Chango's Chicken Shack and several piles of small clean bones which he picked up and moved to one side. The smell of fried chicken clung to the air as he climbed into one of the sleeping bags.

Was he really the Luckiest Boy in the World? Right now, it didn't feel like it. Yes, he was lucky to have woken up before Dr Shard drilled out his brain, and he was lucky to have this den to hide in, but it wasn't exactly the Ritz and he was still on the run.

He was cold too. He dragged the bin liner into which he'd stuffed his extra clothes closer to the sleeping bag. He hadn't had time to see what he was

206

packing; another jumper, one sock, his shorts and a handkerchief. That was hardly going to stave off hypothermia. There were other things inside the sack too. Hecate's revolting collection of anti-ageing potions; jars full of fly-pupae and snakes' eggs; bottles filled with extract of bull's blood; and a soap tin containing the heads of a dozen tiny hummingbirds. Handling them with revulsion, Alfie climbed out of his sleeping bag and piled them in the farthest corner of the den so that he wouldn't have to look at them. When he returned to the sleeping bag, he saw a bundle of papers lying on the ground next to it. On closer inspection he discovered that they were letters tied up with string, eleven of them. Each was written in the same handwriting and addressed to THE PERSON WHO PICKED UP MY BABY. The hairs on the back of Alfie's neck stood to attention. Each letter was the same, but dated one year later than the last.

If you are the good person who took my baby from this bus stop I thank you from the bottom of my heart. People told me I was too young to have a baby and I listened to them, but I was not. Even as I got on the bus I realised I'd made a mistake. I could not bear to be without him. I stopped the bus and ran back to where I left him, but he had gone. I shall leave a letter at the bus stop every year on his birthday in the hope that one day you will see it. If you do, please leave a note for me in the same place, telling me how I might contact you so that I can get my baby back.

Tell my son that I love him and he will always be my baby boy.

x

Eleven years. Eleven letters. Alfie's ears were ringing. Did this mean his aunts weren't really his aunts? Was his only connection to them that they happened to be walking past a bus stop? If they knew his mother wanted him back why didn't they contact her and hand him over? He knew the answer to that question. Because they'd lose their Household Drudge. They'd told him his mother was dead. These letters proved she wasn't. Alfie's hands were stone cold to the very tips of his fingers. She was alive and wanted to know him.

Hearing a scream, Alfie spun round to face the entrance to the den. As he did so he heard feet scampering in the bushes outside. The feet stopped. His heart beat a little bit faster. There was something out there.

Alfie tossed the letters onto the sleeping bag, stepped towards the door and pushed his head outside. If it was an animal, maybe the sight of him would scare it away. But the rustling of dried leaves suggested otherwise. Whatever was out there was trying to circle behind him . . . It had a red tail. Alfie saw a flash through the trees.

It was a werefox! With a red tail and a paw with a white sock. No. Now he could see it properly. It was an ordinary fox. Its narrow, pointed snout; its lips pulled back in a quivering growl, teeth exposed like a picket fence. It was staring straight at him with bright yellow eyes. And then it attacked. It leapt from the cover of the bushes, red tongue lolling, spittle swirling, unafraid of this intruder on its patch.

'WOLFIE!'

The fox pulled up sharply on command and crouched in front of Alfie ready to re-start the attack should it be required.

'Wolfie, what are you doing?'

Fox appeared out of the darkness. In the moonlight, his red coat glowed and its shiny buttons glittered like pearly teeth. Alfie breathed a sigh of relief.

'He thinks you've got Bandit with you,' laughed Fox. 'He's scared. Have you?'

'Got Bandit?' said Alfie. 'No.'

'So what are you doing here?' asked Fox.

'I could ask the same of you.'

'It's *my* den.'

'Yes, but it's two in the morning.'

'We're staying here till that policeman stops looking for us.'

'Is Red with you then?' Alfie asked, peering over Fox's shoulder.

'Somewhere. She goes off walking when she can't sleep. Sometimes she doesn't come back till morning. What about you?'

'Not good.' Alfie explained how Hecate and Mohana had teamed up with Dr Shard and the policeman.

'So you can't go home?'

'Not if I want to keep my brain!' said Alfie. 'You don't know any werefoxes, do you, by any chance?'

'What do you mean?' he asked, stony-faced. Alfie was taken aback.

'Nothing,' he said. 'Just that if you *did* know any werefoxes I could send them up to the house to eat my aunts. That'd teach them.'

'And do you?' said a third voice, drifting round from behind the den.

'Red!' Alfie's heart lifted when he saw her. Her hair was drawn back off her face and bounced against her neck like a bushy red tail.

'Do you know any werefoxes?' she asked

210

her brother. He pulled a face and didn't answer. 'More bad luck, Alfie?' she said, pushing past him and entering the den.

'How did you know that?' he asked.

'I'm guessing you wouldn't be here if it was good.'

'His aunts have teamed up with the mad doctor,' said Fox. 'They tried to eat his brain tonight.'

'Are you serious?' said Red, reappearing in the doorway with Hecate's letters in her hands. 'What are these?' she asked casually.

Alfie had almost forgotten about those letters. Even so, he didn't want anyone else reading them. Not before he knew what he thought about them himself.

'They're just some old letters of my aunts',' he said, grabbing them out of her hand and shoving them up his jumper. Alfie looked at her to see if she'd read them, but found that *she* was staring at *him*. Red turned away when their eyes made contact.

'The brain-eaters obviously didn't succeed then?' she said hurriedly.

'No, that's why I'm here. I needed somewhere safe to hide out for a few days!

'What about the Holiday of Luck thing tomorrow morning?' she asked.

'I can't do that,' said Alfie. 'I'd have to

211

change clothes to do that. And the Prime Minister's sending a limousine at ten-thirty. It would mean going home.'

Red and Fox spoke together.

'You've got to do it.'

'That's your ticket out of here,' explained Red. 'Walk through the traffic in front of millions of people and you'll be famous all over the world.'

'I know that,' said Alfie, 'but . . .'

'But what?' she said. 'If you're famous you can do anything.'

'But what if the Luck Gene's stopped working?'

'Why would it have done that?'

'It can't last for ever,' he said.

'I don't see why not,' she said. 'Your aunts didn't get your brain tonight, did they? You escaped. That was lucky.'

'You bumped into *us*,' said Fox.

'Don't get me wrong,' Alfie said, 'I'm glad to see you, but is that lucky?'

'That depends,' said Red.

'On what?'

'On whether you let us help you or not.'

Alfie wasn't sure what she meant.

'We could be your bodyguards,' she said.

'Bodyguards?'

'Yeah, we'd be good at that,' grinned Fox.

'Doing what?'

212

'Stopping your aunts from nicking your brain before the lucky walk,' Red said, making it sound simple.

'And once you've *done* the walk you'll be free to do what you like,' Fox said. 'You won't need us any more.'

'I still won't have anywhere to live.'

Red ruffled Alfie's hair.

'That will work itself out,' she said, 'but only if you take a chance and make your own luck.'

Everything she said made sense to him, but it was a measure of how suspicious the Luck Gene had made Alfie that he was questioning their motives at all. His aunts turned out not to be his aunts, doctors had proved themselves to be as corruptible as policemen, and even politicians were out for what they could get. Why should he suddenly trust Red and Fox? It wasn't so long ago that Fox had been using him to rob banks. Yes, they'd saved his life, but why?

'If I go along with this you're not going to suddenly turn round and demand half my brain for payment, are you?' Alfie asked sheepishly.

Red folded her arms and looked offended, while Fox just laughed.

'Brains on toast,' he said. 'Have it for breakfast every morning.'

213

'Not everyone's a villain,' Red said. 'Just because me and Fox live unconventionally doesn't make us bad people.' Alfie blushed. Now he felt bad for having mentioned it.

'I know,' he muttered. 'Sorry.'

'It's not a crime to help someone,' she said. 'So here's the deal if you want it. We'll take you back in the morning and hang around while you change and we'll make sure you get into the limousine. There'll be a driver there, so you'll be quite safe. Then we'll meet you in Park Lane for the walk itself. We'll be there with you, every step of the way.'

'I *do* want it,' said Alfie, suitably chastised. 'But how are you going to do it? If anyone recognises you you'll be arrested, and I'm not allowed to take anyone into the VIP area except my close relatives.' How hollow those words sounded now.

'Since when has that ever stopped us?' grinned Fox. 'Cunning's what we are; invisibility's what we do best. There's nowhere me and Red can't go when we're travelling the Stinker. What time does it start?'

'Twelve.'

'We'll be there early,' he said. Fox pushed past into the den to get some sleep, leaving Alfie and Red outside.

'One last thing,' she said. 'When tomorrow's over we need to sit down and take a long hard look at your options, Alfie.'

'Meaning what?' he asked.

'Meaning whatever it means,' she said mysteriously. 'One day at a time, Alfie Pluck. Tomorrow it's enough that your brain is safe in our hands.'

*   *   *

Alfie slept in the den till dawn, when Red and Fox escorted him home to get changed for his lucky walk. They climbed in through Alfie's bedroom window and checked the house for signs of Inspector Champion, Dr Shard and Mr Mulciber. Nothing. Mohana and Hecate remained asleep while Alfie dressed. Then he took them up two cups of tea, and while Red and Fox stood guard on the landing, he drew the curtains.

'The government car will be here in thirty minutes,' he said calmly. 'I'll wait downstairs.' It was as if the night before had never happened.

Thirty minutes later, Alfie jumped into the front seat of the limousine and put his aunts out of reach in the back. The risk of a stiletto being slid between his ribs was

215

small, but his bodyguards had been forthright in their advice.

'Trust no one,' Red had said.

By the time the car pulled away, Fox and Red had already removed the cover from the nearest manhole and were easing themselves down the metal ladder into the sewers.

CHAPTER TWENTY-ONE

While the Holiday of Luck crowds gathered behind the barriers that had been set up along the length of Park Lane, the Quirks were relaxing in the foyer of the Dorchester Hotel. Alfie arrived at eleven with his tasteless aunts in tow, both of whom had dressed for the occasion in shocking-pink wedding cake dresses.

'Good moaning,' said the aliens, speaking as one through their localised vocalised translators. Commander Mmnnaarg, who had spoken so softly to Alfie and the Prime Minister on that first night, hovered forward and threw its tentacles around Alfie's shoulders.

'A word in your shell-suit,' it said secretively. 'As you have probably heard, Alfie, our speck chip has finally been mended. After today's cere-monday we shall be finding the pretty that was left behind in Good Queen Beth's age and going home.'

'So once again I'll be the only creature left on the planet with the Luck Gene inside me,' said Alfie.

'I'm afridge so,' said the alien. 'Assuming, that is, you want to stay.'

Alfie moved the alien away from his aunts who were giggling theatrically behind an aspidistra plant and pretending not to eavesdrop.

'Why wouldn't I stay?' he whispered.

'Well you wouldn't, would you? Not if you came with us,' said the face inside the creature's belly.

'Come with you?' This was not an option Alfie had considered; living in outer space, on a strange planet with aliens who spoke through their belly-buttons. But he'd be a fool to dismiss it right away. After all, Red and Fox couldn't put him up, sleeping in the den was hardly practical and going back to live with Hecate and Mohana, knowing what he now knew about them, was an utter impossibility.

'Don't look so sharked,' said the creature. 'It's lovely on Fortuna. Because we are born with the Luck Gene inside us it never turns bad. Plus it rains chocolate

217

drops and children can choose their own parents.'

Alfie gasped.

'Do I need to give you an answer now?' he asked.

'We'll see you again before we go,' said the alien, smiling. 'Oops, I think that's us!'

A woman wearing headphones and carrying a clipboard was waving the Quirks to the door.

'You're on in five minutes,' she shouted across the foyer. 'Alfie, you're walking in ten!'

Ten minutes to go. Alfie peered out at the crowds. A grandstand had been erected on the pavement by the side of the six-laned road with a small stage at the front, from which Alfie would take his first steps and where Marjorie Lentless was already giving a speech to an audience of journalists and celebrities.

'You can wait round the back of the stage if you like,' said the girl with the clipboard. 'You'll get a better view.'

'Thanks,' he said, leaving the safety of the hotel and wandering outside. His twittering aunts stuck close, as if pinned to his shadow.

*   *   *

218

Marjorie Lentless had talked piffle to the nation ever since the night on top of the O2 Arena when the aliens had walked out of the Shuttle *Relentless*. Now she was piffling some more, gushing modestly about how Marjorie Lentless's Holiday of Luck was her gift to the nation to say thank you for re-electing her. Even as she spoke, she realised her mistake.

'Not that I am making any assumptions,' she laughed. 'Obviously, you, the people, still have to cast your vote in a week's time on Election Day, but I am hopeful that I can count on your support.' Having wriggled out of that one, she tossed an idle speculation into the air and watched it fall like fairy dust. 'May I be honest with you?' she said. 'It has crossed my mind, on several occasions, that maybe *I* have a little bit of the Luck Gene inside *me*, because let's face it, ladies and gentlemen, everything I touch these days just seems to turn to gold!'

The crowd agreed and applauded her for over two minutes.

Then it was time to introduce the Quirks. While Alfie anxiously scanned the crowd for Fox and Red, the Prime Minister thanked the aliens for making the long journey from Fortuna, before presenting each of them with a ceremonial sash. At

the centre of each sash was a gold medal
inscribed with the legend:

BRITISH CITIZENSHIP

ALIEN CLASS

MARJORIE LENTLESS FIXED IT FOR ME!

Alfie watched an ambulance park fifty
yards down from the grandstand, and
sighed. How bizarre life was with the Luck
Gene inside him. Last night he was fleeing
for his life, today he'd been offered a home
on an alien planet. It was certainly
tempting. Choosing his own parents
sounded endlessly pleasing.

'Alfie, we're ready for you now.' The girl
tapped Alfie on the shoulder. 'Are you
nervous?' she asked, as they walked
towards the grandstand where his aunts
were waiting.

'I was,' he said, 'but now I just want to
get on with it.' He stopped suddenly and
pointed at Hecate and Mohana who were
both fidgeting. 'Do you think they are,
though?'

'Nervous?' said the girl with the
clipboard. 'Yes. Their top lips are
sweating.'

'That's what I thought,' said Alfie. 'Now,

why would that be, do you think?'

The girl snorted a laugh.

'I'd have thought that was obvious,' she said. 'Their nephew's about to walk across a road in front of six lanes of moving traffic!'

This was certainly true, but Hecate and Mohana knew that he was the Luckiest Boy in the World. They had no reason to doubt that luck would not guide him safely across. It was Alfie who had doubts; Alfie who should have been nervous; Alfie who had to find the courage to do as Red had told him and 'take a chance'.

He saw Hecate sneak a surreptitious look up Park Lane and followed her gaze to a yellow London cab idling in a taxi rank three hundred yards away. It confirmed his suspicions.

'Where are they?' he muttered, looking around for the two faces he was hoping to see.

*　　　*　　　*

Fox and Red were stuck in the sewers. They had encountered a blockage underneath the Royal Albert Hall. They didn't stop to see what it was, but Fox thought it looked like an opera singer. The important thing was that they were forced

221

to take a detour via Notting Hill and even running fast and skimming across the water, it still added ten minutes to their journey time.

'We're not going to make it!' said Red, panicking as they stopped at a four-way junction. 'Which way now?'

'Right,' shouted Fox. 'That takes us along the top of Hyde Park. When we get to Marble Arch turn right again.'

'I don't have a good feeling about this,' muttered Red as she kicked up her heels.

'Save your breath!' yelled Fox. 'And keep going!'

*   *   *

Back on Park Lane, the Prime Minister was still in full flow. 'And now that we've been into outer space and decorated the Quirks,' she proclaimed, 'it's time to come back down to earth and celebrate our very own National Treasure!'

Hecate and Mohana shoved Alfie in the back and followed him up onto the stage. They had a task to do and they intended to do it.

'Do you think it looks like rain?' Mohana asked her sister loudly so that everybody could hear.

'Hard to say,' replied Hecate.

Alfie looked at them peculiarly. There wasn't a cloud in the sky. What were they up to?

'Oh well,' said Mohana. 'I'll take my umbrella out of my bag just in case.' She pulled out a pink telescopic umbrella and opened it to its full extension.

'So, Alfie, are you ready?'

The Prime Minister was trying her hand at interviewing and had pushed her microphone into Alfie's face.

'Not quite,' he said feebly, procrastinating as best he could to give his bodyguards time to arrive.

'You're not going soft on us now, are you?' she joked for the crowd, who responded with a generous laugh and a ripple of sycophantic applause. 'I'm sure there's nothing to worry about. After all, you are the Luckiest Boy in the World.'

'That may be true,' replied Alfie, 'but I'd like to point out that when the Lucky Hen walked between the cars it got hit.'

'A glancing blow,' scoffed Marjorie Lentless. 'It barely felt it.'

'Yes, but it still got hit,' protested Alfie. 'And if it happens again, it will be *my* legs that snap!'

The Prime Minister did not like Alfie's tone. Any more doubt would take the shine off the spectacle. 'Jolly good,' she said

223

briskly, standing up and smiling. 'Let's get on with it.'

Alfie peeked up the street and was alarmed to see that the yellow cab had started its engine.

'Shall we count him down?'

As the crowd began counting down from 10, Alfie vaguely heard the Prime Minister wishing him luck, but he had stopped listening. The absence of Red and Fox was far more pressing. Maybe their offer of help had been a scam from the off; maybe they were in on the plot too for a fifth of the Luck Gene; maybe *everyone* was playing him for a fool and they were all waiting for him to be hit so they could suck his brains off the tarmac!

'...7...6...5...'

The taxi had pulled out into the traffic but was moving very slowly. Other cars hooted and swerved around it. Would it work if Alfie just put up his hand and said that he needed the loo? That would waste another few minutes...

'...3...2...'

Whatever he did he had better do it fast! But even as he took a step back from the edge he heard Mohana pretend to stumble behind him and felt the tip of her umbrella jab him in the small of his back and propel him off the stage into the maelstrom of

224

traffic.

*   *   *

It was like being trapped in the middle of a stampede of iron bison. Alfie remembered how the Lucky Hen had coped with the clash and thunder around it, by simply walking straight across the road, oblivious to the danger. He attempted to copy her technique. He strolled casually, rolling his hips in an easy gait as if promenading along the seafront without a care in the world. And it worked. The cars avoided him inside his one-man bubble of luck. But he still couldn't get that yellow cab out of his head. The more he thought about it, the more he looked at it, and the more he looked at it, the bigger it became. Closer and closer. As huge as the road itself; as wide as six lanes; unmissable!

Hecate and Mohana watched with glee. The plan was working perfectly. Alfie stood frozen in the middle of the road as the yellow cab accelerated into the third lane and made a beeline for him. Mr Mulciber gripped the steering wheel till his knuckles turned white. There was nothing now between him and his target. That lucky brain was so close he could taste it.

Alfie knew he'd see Mr Mulciber behind

225

the wheel. He was twenty yards away, three seconds from impact. Alfie knew that he would not miss again. He didn't understand why the Luck Gene appeared to work for him one moment and against him the next. All he knew was that seconds from now Alfie Pluck would be obliterated. And in that acceptance came the realisation that he was glad to be going. It must have been the same for the Lucky Hen when Alfie wrung her neck and ate her. Contrary to popular myth, being lucky had brought neither of them anything but misery. In a gesture of surrender, Alfie raised his hands above his head and smiled.

*   *   *

But the Luck Gene had not gone AWOL, nor had it run out of juice. It had simply been biding its time.

The circular cover of a manhole directly in front of Alfie, twisted in the tarmac. It turned in an anti-clockwise direction and lifted up. A grubby face, framed by matted dreadlocks, forced itself through the tiny gap.

'Oi! Alfie!' cried the cheeky voice. 'Told you we'd get here on time.'

In that instant, the front right-hand

wheel of the yellow cab struck the raised manhole cover and diverted the vehicle's trajectory. It veered dramatically to the left and took off across the second lane, across the first lane, across the kerb, across the stage where Alfie had stood seconds earlier, and across the pink screams of Hecate and Mohana Pluck. It took out the sisters with the cold-bloodedness of an executioner's axe, and left them dead on the pavement.

CHAPTER TWENTY-TWO

A joint funeral took place three days later. Identical pink hearses carrying identical pink coffins covered in identical pink flowers arranged into the identical shapes of two pink flamingos. The message on the card pinned to the beak of each flamingo was identical too: TO MY DEAR SISTER. SORRY YOU'RE DEAD. LOVE, YOUR SISTER. Hecate and Mohana had never had any friends but each other, and they had written the cards themselves twenty years earlier.

Little wonder then that Alfie was the only person in attendance. He had deliberately chosen not to wear black, because that would have implied he was sad and he wasn't. He was extremely happy. It was just him, the vicar and a gravedigger, who fell asleep during the committal.

Alfie was puzzled as to what happened now. Did he have to move out of the house? Did he have any money? Had the aunts written a will? Not that he expected to be left anything. After all, he now knew he wasn't related to Hecate and Mohana, he was just their slave. But the Luck Gene was still functioning, so maybe that would work in his favour. The one thing he regretted was that he'd never had the chance to ask his aunts where that bus stop was. At least it would have given him somewhere to start looking for his mother.

*　　　*　　　*

As Alfie tossed a handful of dirt onto the lid of each coffin, a woman marched across the cemetery towards him. She was wearing a suit and carrying a black leather briefcase. She announced herself in a no-nonsense way that made Alfie step back and slip on a gravestone.

'I'm from Social Services,' she said. 'I'm sure you've been expecting me.'

Alfie hadn't been expecting anyone.

'No,' he said warily. 'Is Social Services what I think it is?'

'What do you think it is?' she replied.

Alfie shrugged. It wasn't just *one* thing.

'Fast cars,' he said. 'Guns, motorboats, submarines, micro-light aircraft, snakes in the shower, kissing and death.'

'Well that's quite an extreme view of what we do,' she said. 'I mean we do encounter all of those things in the course of our duty, but not every day.'

'Oh, I see,' he said. 'You're the backroom people who make the exploding pens and spectacles that fire acid at Russian thugs.'

'Ah, I think you may be confusing us with the *Secret* Service,' she said. 'We're *Social* Services. We find children foster homes.'

'Foster homes!' The possibility of being sent to a foster home had never crossed his mind. Living with complete strangers was not Alfie's idea of a lucky break.

'I'm here to take you away,' she said. 'Now that you have nobody to look after you, I've got no choice but to put you into care.'

Having just regained his freedom, Alfie was not about to give it up lightly. He had to fight, to convince this do-gooder that he was capable of looking after himself.

'If I was a normal eleven-year-old,' he

said, trying to sound reasonable, 'I'd agree with you, but I'm not.' He pointed to the holes in the ground. 'I've been cooking and cleaning for them all my life. I know how to do it. I can wash clothes, shop, lay a fire and I'm brilliant at filling a bath with hot mud.'

'Actually,' she said firmly, 'I'm not *asking* you, Alfie, I'm *telling* you.'

'But I'm lucky,' he complained. A wave of panic raised the timbre of his voice to a squeal. 'You know I am. There's nobody luckier. I'm like a cat. I always fall on my feet. So you're quite safe to leave me where I am.' He could see that his words were having no effect. She smiled that smile that grown-ups did when they'd already made up their mind.

'Being lucky is not enough, I'm afraid. We need to know that there is someone taking care of your everyday needs.'

In desperation, Alfie scraped the barrel of lost causes. 'The Prime Minister's a personal friend,' he cried.

But the woman even had an answer to that.

'She's a bit busy right now, Alfie. And between you and me, I don't think you'd be that happy with her. She doesn't strike me as the maternal type.'

It didn't matter what Alfie said, he

couldn't find the key to unlock this woman's flinty heart. He needed a truth that was so irrefutable it would trump every argument she had prepared, and when he realised what it was, it stopped her in her tracks.

'But I've already got a mother,' he said. 'I just haven't found her yet.'

'Don't lie,' the woman replied, not knowing quite how to respond to this new information.

'I'm not lying,' he protested. 'I've got the letters to prove it. Those old ladies weren't my real aunts. They found me at a bus stop and stole me to be their slave!'

But arguing simply made things worse.

Now I *know* you're lying!'

Angrily, the woman snatched a pen from her top pocket and took a form from her briefcase, which she signed with a triumphant flourish.

That was it then. Deal done.

Frustrated, Alfie pushed his arms out in front of him, made a fist with each hand and pressed them together. 'What are you doing?' she asked.

'For the handcuffs,' he said dramatically. 'You can take me away now.'

'What's going on?'

Alfie and the woman from Social Services turned to see a young woman with long red hair and a boy with matted dreadlocks, which, for once, had been gathered into a pony tail. Around the tops of their arms were black armbands made from strips of plastic bin liner.

'Sorry we're late,' said the boy. 'I was taking a shower.'

'Are you ready to go home now, Alfie?'

The young woman with red hair spoke in a gentle voice and held out her hand to lead Alfie away, but the woman from Social Services intervened.

'Who are you?' she said officiously, adding with a sneer, 'his mother?'

'She's my sister, Red,' answered Fox.

'Alfie lives with us,' Red said.

This was news to Alfie. Was she being serious? She certainly wasn't smiling.

'And I'm Fox, Alfie's best friend.'

What was going on?

Red reached past the woman and took Alfie's hand. 'Have we finished?' she asked.

'No,' said the official, waving the form in the air. 'There are certain criteria I need to satisfy before I can even *think* about closing this case.'

'Good,' said Red who had filled out similar forms many times. 'Write this down. I have a permanent job at Chango's Chicken Shack and a flat above the shop with electricity, running water, a proper toilet and an oven which sometimes I open up and put food inside to cook.'

The woman cleared her throat.

'If you think this is a joke,' she said, 'you're very much mistaken.'

'I don't,' said Red. 'The roof doesn't leak, the walls are dry and the bugs know better than to bother us. And five times a week, every morning from Monday to Friday in fact, my brother gets up and goes to school. Actually no, that's a lie.' Scenting a chink in Red's armour, the woman looked up sharply from the form. 'Sometimes he doesn't want to get up, so I have to wake him and force him out of the door. Anything else?'

While the woman phoned her office to report these unexpected developments, a startled Alfie pulled Red and Fox aside.

'What are you doing?' he asked.

'We were coming up here to surprise you,' Red said, 'but when I heard what this woman was threatening to do, I just blurted it out.'

Alfie still couldn't get things straight in his head. 'You're saying I can stay with you?'

'If you want,' she said. 'It's not a big deal.'

It was to Alfie. The last people he'd lived with had lied to him all his life. And being the Luckiest Boy in the World, people wanted to know him for all sorts of odd reasons, and not all of them friendship. And then there was the dark side of the Luck Gene, the part that scared him. He wouldn't want to inflict that on anyone.

'You don't know what it's like living with me,' he said.

'Good for getting chicken,' chuckled Fox.

'Have you never heard Dr Shard's warning?' Alfie said. 'When good luck dances into a room, bad luck is never far behind, swishing its bushy tail of death.'

Fox scratched a scab on the top of his head. 'What does that mean?'

'Being the Luckiest Boy in the World can sometimes be great, but other times . . .' Alfie shrugged, '. . . well you saw what that cab did to my aunts.'

'They weren't your aunts,' said Red emphatically. 'And that wasn't bad luck.'

'It was for *them.*'

'But not for *you,*' Red assured him. 'It was good luck for you; *great* luck; *stupendous* luck; mega, breathtaking, out of this world, *incredible* luck!'

'It was, wasn't it,' grinned Alfie, suddenly looking puzzled. 'How did you know they weren't my aunts?' he asked Red. There was a brief hiatus while she blushed and realised she'd said too much.

'I read those letters.' She grimaced. 'That night in the den. Sorry.' Alfie was expecting it to matter, but it didn't. Red and Fox had offered to share their home. That was what mattered to Alfie.

The woman finished her call to the office and came over with her news.

'My boss says he knows you,' she said, poking Fox in the chest. 'He says you're the feral kid who lives on the common.' 'It's just a camp,' said Fox.

'Sometimes,' said Alfie, entering the spirit of the game, 'if we can't sleep, we all go up there and walk around a bit, that's all.'

Alfie avoided catching Fox's eye while he was lying just in case it showed in his face.

'None of us actually lives there,' said Red. 'What sort of people do you think we are?'

The woman from Social Services couldn't answer that question without resorting to insult. Officious and petty-minded she might have been, but she was never rude.

'Fine,' she said, popping the form back into her briefcase and snapping the lock shut. 'In that case, I'm happy. Are you sure this is what you want, Alfie?'

'It is,' he said, beaming.

'Very well.'

She spun on her heel, then paused fleetingly and with her back still turned, said, 'It would seem as if you *are* the Luckiest Boy in the World after all.'

*   *   *

Several crows sat in the woody fingers of the trees and formed a guard of honour as Alfie and his new flatmates left the cemetery. As they approached the iron gates with the gilded cherubs on, Fox stopped walking and sniffed, wrinkling his nose in disgust.

'Can you smell bad eggs?' he asked.

'Eggs!' gasped Alfie. His flesh shuddered as he swung around to check behind him.

'What's the matter?' asked Red.

'Did either of you see what happened to the cab driver who killed my aunts?'

Even as he asked the question, the earth opened up in front of them. It plunged away into a hole as deep and wide as a grave, and out of it shot two wailing zombies. Their white, marzipan flesh was covered in mud and they groaned gruesomely.

Red was the first to scream, but Fox and Alfie were not far behind. It was only when

Fox spotted the spring-loaded seesaw underneath the zombies' backs and the snorkels and masks they were wearing to help them breathe underground that he smelled a rat.

In the split second before Fox recognised the zombies, the taller of the two, the one with steel-capped teeth, lunged forward and grabbed Alfie, lifting him off the ground so that his legs thrashed uselessly in the air.

As Red and Fox stepped forward to snatch Alfie back, the sound of a gun being cocked in their ears stopped them in their tracks.

'Back up!' shouted the familiar voice of Inspector Champion (retired). The two zombies removed their masks as the ex-policeman stepped alongside them.

'I knew that stink was you!' grunted Alfie, squirming to look up at his captor's face.

'Of course it's us,' said Dr Shard, his head twitching like a chicken's. 'Who else hates you more? Nobody. But then nobody has *cause* to hate you more than I!' The doctor's face had inflated with rage. 'You steal my life's work and refuse to give it back. You are *my* creation, Alfie Pluck. If I choose to destroy you I can!'

'How many times . . . I wish I never had

eaten that Luck Gene, but I *did!*'

'An eat for an eat!' cackled the doctor. 'Your brain is toast, Alfie!'

Dr Shard jerked his head skyward as a helicopter appeared over the church steeple and landed in the field on the other side of the cemetery wall. He slapped Mr Mulciber's arms and they backed towards the landing pad leaving the Inspector as a first line of defence.

'In case you're thinking of jumping me,' warned the armed man, pointing the weapon at Red and Fox, 'it's only fair to warn you that I won a gold rosette on the firing range at Hendon. Top of my year. And this gun is loaded.'

'What did I ever do to *you* to turn you bad?' shouted Alfie at Inspector Champion.

'If it hadn't been for you, Alfie, my reputation would still be intact and I would still have a pension,' said the Inspector bitterly. 'Your antics have cost me everything.'

'Your brain will feed us all!' taunted Mr Mulciber, rolling Alfie onto the floor of the helicopter and jumping in behind him. 'Shame we missed in Park Lane,' he shouted.

'But we won't miss again,' promised Dr Shard, as he hurled his twisted frame towards the hatch and dragged himself aboard as well.

As the helicopter rotor blades increased in speed for take off and the Inspector turned his back to board, Red and Fox rushed towards it, yelling, 'Jump, Alfie! Jump!'

But a dead weight, called Mr Mulciber, was sitting on the boy's legs. The helicopter lurched to the right as it lifted into the air, throwing the ex-policeman across one of the seats and knocking the gun out of his hand.

'We'll find you, Alfie!' hollered Red.

'I doubt it,' shouted Mr Mulciber, snatching the gun off the floor and letting loose a couple of shots in the general direction of the ground. He fired randomly, but one of the shots found a target. A cherub's leg was shattered by the bullet and the cast iron sculpture fell forward off the gate, striking Red a heavy blow across her temple.

Alfie sat up. Through the open hatch he watched her fall to her knees. Her head slumped forward and her chin pressed down into her chest.

'RED!'

'She'll be all right!' yelled Fox, wrapping his arms around his sister. 'Just trust in the luck, Alfie. Trust in the luck!'

And as the helicopter fell upwards into

the sky, Alfie watched in amazement as Red lifted her head and her eyes seemed to glow like two yellow moons.

CHAPTER TWENTY-THREE

The inside of the helicopter had been converted into an In-Flight Operating Theatre. Dr Shard reasoned that nobody could stop him extracting Alfie's brain while he was floating around in the sky. Superman, perhaps, but how likely was that?

'It's showtime!' Mr Mulciber grinned moronically as Dr Shard snapped on his surgical rubber gloves. He licked his lips and pretended to eat an imaginary frontal lobe, cramming it into his mouth like a slice of juicy watermelon. 'Mmmmmm! Delicious brain!'

Alfie had been in this situation before and escaped with his life. He wanted to believe that something extraordinary would happen again to save him. Quite what that would be was another matter. A flock of birds flying through the engine, an electrical storm, a pilot with food poisoning? It was hard keeping faith with the Luck Gene when he was strapped to a makeshift operating table with three deranged men stood over him, intent on extracting his brain. Nonetheless, he decided to hold his nerve and taunt them. Anything to delay the first thrust of that oscillating probe.

'Just thought I should remind you, in case any of you've forgotten, that I'm the Luckiest Boy in the World,' he said, smiling.

'It can't last for ever!' sneered Mr Mulciber, with the swagger of a man who thought himself invincible.

'Is that what you think too?' Alfie teased the Inspector, who was coping unsuccessfully with a bout of air-sickness and was scared to open his mouth for fear of what might come out.

'Hold your tongue,' ordered Dr Shard, 'or I'll cut it out.' His twitching had spread to his left eyelid, which was now blinking hard and fast.

'Just one more thing and then I'll be quiet,' Alfie said. He sounded remarkably calm, which was a result of his most recent insight into the Luck Gene. 'Imagine how much luck an egg requires to survive a fall from the top of a tower block,' he said. 'Now imagine this . . . each and every egg produced by the Lucky Hen who gave me her gene survived that fall. That means

241

luck triumphed every single time. It *never* failed.' Alfie could see in the furrowed brows louring over him that his speech had hit its mark. 'Start your probe by all means, but don't be surprised when it brings all sorts of bad things crashing down on your heads!'

The doubt was enough to make Mr Mulciber look out of the window for any airborne hiccups that might thwart their plan, and for Dr Shard to make one final jittery sweep of the cabin. At last, when he was satisfied that there was nothing the Luck Gene could do to save Alfie, he flicked the switch on the side of the handle and the high-speed oscillating ear probe buzzed into life.

The one place they hadn't checked was above.

The helicopter shuddered like a seal in the jaws of a killer whale and the rotor blade stopped instantly. The three men were blown across the cabin like chaff in a twister and before they could stand up again, the top of the helicopter was prised open with what could only be described as a giant can opener.

A metal claw dropped down through the hole and scooped up the operating table with Alfie still on it. Dr Shard, Mr Mulciber and Inspector Champion could

242

not believe their eyes.

*   *   *

Above the helicopter, piggy-back style, hovered the Quirk space ship. Having been fixillated in the Garage Cortex of the aliens' minds, it had been returned to the real world and was once again visible. Like an eagle with its paralysed prey, it carried the stricken helicopter out to the west of London and dropped it into one of the Staines Reservoirs, where it lay briefly on top of the water like a dead fish then slowly sank.

'That should teach them a bassoon they won't regret,' laughed Commander Mmnnaarg through its localised vocalised translator, as every alien on the flight deck applauded the helicopter's splash down. Their tentacles made a wet slappy noise that brought to mind sea lions enjoying the opera.

Alfie could not thank the Quirk Commander enough.

'Our peashooter,' the alien said. 'And welcome abroad. You are among friends here, Alfie Pluck.'

'So I can see,' said the boy as he swung his legs off the operating table. 'You just saved my life.'

'Well we couldn't very well fly off and leave one of our own to diet, could we?'

Alfie was intrigued.

'Am I one of *you* then?' he asked, adding excitedly, 'Am I the pretty you left behind in Good Queen Bess's reign?'

'Not extremely,' came the jumbled reply. 'You're more of an honorary member.'

'Since I ate that chicken?'

'No,' corrected a shy voice from the bridge. 'Before that.'

The new voice caused the deck to fall silent and Alfie was suddenly aware that the aliens were all smiling at him. 'What is it?' he said self-consciously.

'I'd like you to meet Doggo,' said Commander Mmnnaarg. 'He has something to tell you.'

The alien who had just spoken increased the rotations of the tripodal structure underneath its skirt and floated across the synthetic stone floor towards Alfie. It stopped in front of the boy and hovered like a ghost.

'Do you remember the day you got your dog?' it asked in perfect English.

'Like it was yesterday,' said Alfie, looking around the flight deck for a clue as to what was going on. 'I found Bandit at the bottom of the garden.'

'And have you ever wondered how he

244

came to be there?'

'He dug under the fence I think.'

'I mean, why he chose *you?*'

This was a strange question. 'No,' said Alfie.

He paused briefly to follow a thought.

'Do you know where Bandit is?' he asked slowly.

By way of a reply the alien pushed its face up against the translucent wall of its stomach. Alfie squeaked with disbelief.

'Bandit?' he gasped. 'Is that you or have you been eaten by this alien?'

'It's me,' said Bandit. 'I *am* an alien. I've been reunited with my own kind and taken on my old form, although a bit of me seems to be stuck.'

'You've still got the face of a boxer?'

'Yes,' said the dog-alien. 'My Quirk face won't come back.'

Even to Alfie, who had seen some strange stuff in the last few weeks, this was pretty weird. Nonetheless he couldn't stop himself from throwing his arms around his old friend and hugging him till his jelly wobbled.

After a nice cup of sweet tea to offset Alfie's shock, Bandit explained what had happened. He related how a freak accident had left a Quirk stranded on Earth in 1588, the year of the Spanish Armada. It had

245

hidden in some woods in Richmond and only come out for food at night when there was nobody around. Some peasants had seen it and told the army that there was a dangerous creature living in the trees— probably a Spaniard, they thought. That was it, the Quirk had to change its appearance immediately or be captured and killed.

'Quirks can change their appearance once in their lifetime,' clarified Bandit. 'I chose to become a boxer. Unfortunately because of my tripodal structure I could only generate three legs, but the face was a good enough match. From then on, every ten years or so, I regenerated as a puppy and had to run away to find a new home.'

'And that's how you found me?'

'Yes,' said Bandit. 'It was pure luck.'

Alfie's mind raced back through some of the adventures that he and Bandit had shared.

'So when that elephant sat on the fence and neither of us got hurt that was the Luck Gene working in *both* of us?' he deduced.

'Precisely.'

'And Talullah, the three legged greyhound, is she a Quirk too?'

'No, she's a *real* greyhound who happens to only have three legs.'

'Then why did you go with her and leave

246

me?'

'I didn't have a choice. If I hadn't gone with her and had some puppies I would have looked like a fraud.'

'You've got puppies?'

'Just the one,' said Bandit, 'and even *I* think it looks strange.'

As he spoke a tiny three-legged dog with the head of a boxer, the body of a greyhound, and the legs of a Quirk came sliding across the floor at Alfie, yapping for all it was worth. He scooped it up into his arms and held it tight as it washed his face and explored the inside of his nose with its pink tongue.

'I think it likes you,' laughed Bandit, as the Quirk Commander put a paternal tentacle around Alfie's shoulder.

'Which brings us onto the rail raisin we dragged you up here in the first plate,' he said solemnly. 'Alfie Pluck, we are waiting for your answer.'

Alfie had known this would come up eventually. They had asked him to go home to Fortuna with them and he still hadn't replied. Whatever he decided he knew he couldn't win. In front of him sat Bandit, his best friend, willing him to say yes, but back on earth there was Red and Fox who'd asked him to live with them and a mother just waiting to be found. Twenty-

247

four hours earlier, with nothing to keep him on earth, he'd have said yes to the Quirks. But now he had the chance to be part of a real family with people he could already call friends.

'I don't think I can,' he said softly, unable to look Bandit in the eyes. 'Not that you're not all lovely,' he added guiltily, 'but I've only just discovered that I've got a mother. And I'd never forgive myself if I didn't at least try to find her.' The aliens looked crestfallen.

It was Bandit who spoke first.

'Of course, if you stayed,' he said, 'I wouldn't be able to stay with you. A Quirk can only alter its appearance once in its lifetime and now that I've changed back, that's it for good. But you could keep the puppy, I suppose.'

'Could I?' blurted Alfie excitedly.

'I don't see why not. He can protect you from all those nasty Earthlings.'

And so by common consent it was decided. Alfie would go back and live with Red and Fox, and the puppy, which Alfie had now named Lucky, would go with him. All that remained was for Alfie to say his goodbyes and for the Quirks to return him to Earth so he could begin the rest of his life.

Unfortunately the drop-off did not go

according to plan. The Quirk operating the Molecular Transporter was so moved by Alfie and Bandit's farewell that instead of inputting the co-ordinates for Chango's Chicken Shack, 61458329, she was all tentacles and suckers, and inputted 61548320. Alfie found himself standing on top of a tower block in Staines, and the sight of an alien space craft hovering just above the building, like a big pointy finger in the sky proclaiming ALFIE IS HERE, had attracted three unwanted visitors. As Alfie materialised on the flat roof, who should come bursting through the Fire Exit door, but the sodden figures of Dr Shard, Mr Mulciber and Inspector Champion (retired).

Alfie was unfazed.

'Now I know this looks bad,' he whispered to the puppy that was tucked up tight inside his jumper. 'But just watch how lucky I am!'

*   *   *

The first bit of luck was that Inspector Champion (retired) was in no mood for a fight. Despite being a hunky, chunky sort of chap the flight in the helicopter and subsequent swim in Staines Reservoir had left him feeling as sick as a dog. He had picked up a rather unpleasant infection in the water. A fluke worm had taken up residence in his gut, from where, for the next twenty years, it would produce millions and millions of tiny fluke worms that would swim around his stomach behaving like vandals. This meant that the next twenty years would be rather unpleasant for Inspector Champion (retired), who would have to spend at least fourteen hours a day on the lavatory.

But one down still left two standing. Dr Shard and Mr Mulciber squelched across the roof towards Alfie like a couple of pumped-up wrestlers.

'It's fitting, don't you think,' crowed the blinking Dr Shard, 'that my quest for the Luck Gene *began* on a roof and will shortly *end* on one too.'

Alfie backed up as far as he dared. There was no rail around the edge of the roof; just a straight drop to the ground, past sixty-four floors of office retail space . . . and the gap between him and his would-be assassins was closing.

'The thing that has always intrigued me,' said the doctor, 'is what would happen if I threw a lucky boy off the top. Everyone knows that lucky eggs don't break, but boys . . . I wonder. Would their heads smash open on the pavement or not?'

'Not mine,' said Alfie. 'I'll show you.'

A quick glance over his shoulder told him there was a cable twenty feet down from the rooftop which connected his building to the next. With the help of the Luck Gene, he would jump across, catch it and swing down to the ground. Smiling at Dr Shard and Mr Mulciber, he leapt over the edge.

As the wind whistled past his ears he patted Lucky on the head.

'Don't worry,' he said, 'it's all under control.' Holding the puppy tight with his left hand he reached out for the cable with his right. Unfortunately the cable bashed into the back of his hand and bounced right off. Alfie continued to fall. He could hear the voices of Dr Shard and Mr Mulciber howling their revenge from the rooftop.

'Who's lucky now!' they yelled, bursting into an uncontrolled peal of maniacal laughter.

Alfie didn't know what had gone wrong.

'I'm so sorry,' he shouted at Lucky against the noise of the rushing wind. 'We could have been sitting on Fortuna now enjoying a shower of chocolate buttons. Instead I've rather stupidly gone and chosen death by tall building.'

This was it. Seconds left. The end.

Incredibly, a flat bed lorry carrying trampolines for a new Gymnastics Hall in Brentford was just parking up in front of the building and Alfie and Lucky landed right on top. The combined elasticity of twelve stacked trampolines absorbed the velocity of Alfie's descent and converted the downward energy into take off. He shot back up the building faster than he had fallen and flew past the astonished faces of Dr Shard and Mr Mulciber, who, looking up to watch their indestructible nemesis fly past, lost their balance and toppled off themselves. Alfie landed back on the roof and immediately peered over the edge to see where his adversaries had gone. Somehow Mr Mulciber had managed to clasp onto the cable with his metal teeth and Dr Shard had managed to grip onto the bottom of Mr Mulciber's trousers with his hands. They were hanging over a concrete gorge screaming, or rather Dr Shard was screaming, because Mr Mulciber would have dropped them both if he'd opened his mouth.

'Don't let go, Mr Mulciber! Do NOT let go! Can you just nibble your way along the cable? A bit to our left. The lorry's still there. If we can just edge along a fraction I think we'll hit the trampolines.'

Mr Mulciber grunted something unintelligible.

'Can't understand you,' yelled the doctor. 'I hope that cable's a telephone wire and not a high-voltage electricity pylon, because if your metal teeth were to bite through the insulation and make contact with the electricity I think we could be electrocuted rather badl—'

He never finished his sentence, because there was a loud explosion followed by a brilliant flash. When Alfie opened his eyes, the smoke was just clearing to reveal a rather gruesome sight. Still hanging from the cable like a Christmas decoration from Hell, Dr Shard and Mr Mulciber were fried in the sky, charred black like a pair of burnt chicken wings from Chango's Chicken Shack.

Alfie covered Lucky's eyes.

'Come on,' he said. 'Let's go home.'

CHAPTER TWENTY-FOUR

Home was a one-bedroomed flat above the chicken shop. Fox, Alfie and Lucky shared a bed, while on the other side of the room, separated only by a sack curtain, slept Red. She was asleep when Alfie turned up and stayed that way for another twenty-four hours. When she finally woke she showed no ill-effects from her bump on the head.

'It was just a graze,' she said bravely, showing Alfie the faintest of pink scars on her temple.

That night, they ate fried chicken as Alfie told them the story of his life, starting with his evil aunts, his years as their slave and their terrifying tales about werefoxes. He told them about the Prime Minister and the aliens who shared their genetic material with him, about falling from a great height and the elephant that sat on the fence. But above all he told them about Lucky's father, Bandit, who turned out to be the wackiest dog in the universe.

'So what's the verdict,' asked Red as she put the boys to bed. 'Is the Luck Gene a good thing or bad?'

'Both,' said Alfie.

'No, you have to choose!' shouted Fox.

'OK,' said Alfie playing along. 'On balance, I'd say . . Good.'

'So you'd recommend it?' asked Red.

'Why?' said Alfie. 'Are you planning to take it?' Alfie meant it as a joke and Fox and Red took it as such. Five minutes later, when the lights went off, Alfie and Fox were still laughing.

*   *   *

Alfie drifted into a dream. He was walking Lucky across the common throwing a stick for him to fetch. Lucky ran behind a bush and didn't come back. After searching for the puppy up trees and down holes, Alfie sat on a bench, because he was tired. Next to his elbow was a rubbish bin full of cooked chicken carcasses and crumpled napkins oozing grease. And then it was dark. The air was full of children's screams. Alfie had fallen asleep and now sat up full of fear. The bench was no longer hard. It was soft and warm and looking at him with a pair of yellow eyes. It was a huge fox wearing a red and green uniform. It had a chicken under one leg, and under the other a wriggling child. It flashed a cunning smile at Alfie before curling its tail around his body and squeezing him till his buttons burst.

Alfie woke with a start. He was curled up inside the twisted sheet. The bedroom was dark and for a moment he struggled to remember where he was. A scream from the common brought his dream flooding back. He shivered. That was the first dream he had ever had about werefoxes. The first was bad. *The first meeting with a werefox will be in a dream. The second will be in the flesh when it eats you.* Wasn't that what his aunts had always told him? The screaming continued.

'Did you hear that?' Alfie whispered to Fox.

Another scream.

'Fox?' Alfie kicked his leg across the bed and was horrified to feel . . . nothing. Fox had gone.

There was a third scream from the common and Alfie sat up.

He slid out of bed and groped around in the dark for his clothes. Why hadn't he put two and two together before he moved in? Of course Fox was a werefox — the name, the fleas, the mange, the love of chicken, the restlessness at night . . . Alfie had walked *himself* into the werefox's den. Like a chicken to the slaughter.

'What are you doing?'

The curtain was pulled back and an underpowered bulb on the landing cast a soft light behind Fox's head. 'Are you getting dressed?'

Alfie hurriedly pulled his trousers on so that he was ready to run if he had to.

'Where've you been?' he asked Fox accusingly.

256

'Loo,' said Fox falling back onto the mattress. 'The flush doesn't work.' He yawned widely. 'Where are you going?'

Alfie calmed down. He was over-reacting. He needed to give his imagination a rest.

'The loo too,' he said.

It flushed first time.

As Alfie tiptoed back through Red's side of the room, he saw that she was not in her bed.

Fox poked his head through the room divider.

'What are you thinking about?' he said. 'You look worried.'

'Red's not here?'

'No. She's out.'

'Out?'

Alfie's head was full of unwanted images; a pointed black nose nuzzling a sea of frothing blood; a hairy, yellow-eyed creature howling at the moon. He had to ask the next question. He didn't want to hear the answer, but he had to ask it.

'On the common?'

His heart was pounding.

'It's hard to say where she is,' Fox said. 'She's a restless soul at night. Sometimes she goes to the common, other times she goes to a bus shelter in Peckham.'

It was as if Alfie had just received an

electric shock. 'A bus shelter?'

How could an object as ordinary as a bus shelter pick up a person's life, shake it and put it back upside-down? This one had. Could it possibly be that Red was Alfie's long-lost mother? If so, why hadn't the Luck Gene let him know earlier? Alfie knew why. Because it had a twist up its sleeve; it *always* had a twist up its sleeve. Good luck had to be balanced with bad. That was the golden rule. Well, Alfie was fed up with it. After all that he'd been through, why couldn't the Luck Gene, just this once, leave him alone to enjoy his life? Instead it continued to tease him: 'Alfie, meet your mother. Oh, by the way, she's a child-chomping werefox.'

It was never going to end, was it? He couldn't say Doctor Shard hadn't warned him.

When good luck danced into a room, bad luck was never far behind, swishing its-bushy tail of death.

And now that Alfie knew this to be true, he would find a way to cope.

ENDNOTE

At the time of going to press, Alfie Pluck has still not been knighted. This is hardly surprising, because the woman who was going to knight him is no longer Prime Minister. The gruesome deaths of Hecate and Mohana on live, prime time television shocked the nation. The people held Marjorie Lentless responsible, and as a result did not re-elect her.

About the Author

For twenty five years, Jamie Rix has combined a career in television as a director, writer and producer with writing for children. He has worked on a wide variety of comedy programmes including the BAFTA winning The Revenge Files of Alistair Fury and Grizzly Tales for Gruesome Kids, as well as the British Comedy Award winning Faith in the Future and most recently the BBC sitcoms My Hero and Not Going Out. He continues writing for television and film, as well as writing books for children of all ages.

Acknowledgements

My father-in-law, John Middleton Murry, was a highly accomplished novelist who also wrote science fiction under the pseudonym, Richard Cowper. Just before he died he took me aside and said, 'I've long had this idea about a scientist who invents the Luck Gene by dropping eggs off a tall building. I'm never going to use the idea now, so if you want it you can have it.'

It was the most unusual present I have ever been given. I sat on the idea for eight years, boring my wife Helen with many different permutations of the story, until I had worked out how to use it. I hope I've used it well and that John would have approved.

Apart from John and Helen, I would also like to thank my agent Lindsey Fraser and my editor Jenny Glencross who both put countless hours of labour into the final manuscript.